Content Warning: This is a fictional work of .... However, in the interest of public safety and social responsibility within the community, the publisher of this book has included a content warning. It is the readers duty to familiarize themselves with this books content by reading this content warning before reading this book. 1. A trigger or content warning has been included to warn people about content that might elicit a strong or potentially harmful emotional response in certain people, but which others might find benign. Because the severity of response, and the opinions of what constitutes offensive material may vary amongst the public, and is wholly subjective, no differentiation between 'content' and 'trigger warning' has been made on this warning. It encompasses both, as the subjects could experience both or neither depending on the person. 2. The Leopold Bloom Press has included this content warning to enable readers to identify content in advance that may be unsuitable for them, so that they can make informed choices about what they chose to read, and to ensure that those who are particularly sensitive to triggers can chose not to engage with potentially upsetting reading material. 3. The Leopold Bloom Press wishes to advise those prone to anxiety, mental health issues or who are triggered by the mention of eating disorders, historical events of an upsetting nature, agism, bullying or any other potentially upsetting material that may arise in fictionalized scenarios in this book, or any other personal interpretation or opinion about this content, to consider avoiding this novel. 4. The Leopold Bloom Press expressly states that the inclusion of a content warning is not a judgement about the existence of said content. Nor does it offer a barometer to measure the level of upset which this fictional story may or may not induce in some readers. 5. Any topic raised in this book is done so because the writer and publisher consider it a necessary part of the artistic expression and a necessary part of the narrative context. This content warning has been included to help some readers veer away from material that may affect them negatively. It is the readers responsibility to read this content warning in advance of reading this title, to adhere to the advice given herein, to consider the risks of reading this material to them personally, and to avoid this book if they feel that they might be affected by it. 6. If you have been affected by any of the issues mentioned above, or those raised in this fictional novel, or if you are particularly sensitive to emotional reactions, it is advisable not to read this book, and to contact an appropriate licensed professional counsellor, or physician. The Leopold Bloom Press expressly recommends the reader to discontinue reading this material if anxiety or any other triggers result, and to seek professional care immediately. The Leopold Bloom Press does not accept responsibility, offer refunds, reimbursements or engage in any discussion or process with parties who read this book and become triggered, or emotionally destabilized, angered or upset by the fictional narrative herein. 7. Every effort has been made to achieve accuracy, however historians, educators, academics or those seeking scientific quantifiable facts around actual topics reflected in this fictional story should consult non-fictional works. 8. This story is not about the writer, publisher, other writers, historic figures, places , organizations, media or any other person or institute. It is artwork, a work of fiction. In no way does any part of this book or story reflect the actual views of the writer or publisher, or persons known to them or if mentioned the actual places, media outlets, business, city, or otherwise.

Writing Man by Frances Flannery

THE LEOPOLD BLOOM PRESS

First published in Ireland in 2022 by The Leopold Bloom Press.

ISBN (PB) 9781739772703, ISBN (E) 9781739772710

Contents

Chapter 1

Katzback, Frankfurt, Germany

Amidst the unspeakable horrors of a concentration camp, a young woman hunches over a scrapbook, the nib of her makeshift pen scratching softly as she writes. Her manuscript is her only comfort. She has filled it with beautiful, uplifting tales of the loveliest aspects of a world that still exists in her memory.

Outside, a cold wind howls, carrying with it the distant echoes of suffering. Inside, surrounded by the stench of death and stripped of everything she once held dear, the words she pens are a defiance against the darkness. Her words have great power, the power to transport her away from her grim reality, even if just for a moment. But someone has informed on her. Here, it is forbidden to entertain such fanciful ideas.

A sudden noise outside makes her jump. She pauses, her hand trembling slightly as she listens. The heavy boots of soldiers echo in the corridor, getting closer. Panic surges through her. She hurriedly folds the manuscript, her fingers deftly tucking it under the thin, lice-ridden mattress of her bed. The sound of the door being forced open is followed by the blinding beam of a flashlight.

"Come," says a sharp voice. "Now!" As she is led away that fateful night, she has no idea that her stories will change the world in ways she could never have anticipated through the most unlikely of people.

Now the year is 1986. Earlier Tobias Pilzerhoff attended a recital at the Goethe University Frankfurt in honor of his father where a young professor had flirted with him, but Tobias was not tempted off course. Tonight, he is to attend a writing class, where he might get the chance to flaunt his own literary knowledge. As he puts the finishing touches to his outfit, he considers himself in the mirror: a slim, blonde-haired, tall young man, handsome except for the shadows around his eyes and a mildly mean dip to the corner of his mouth. His mustard corduroy trousers are pressed. His brown leather brogues and belt are of the highest quality leather. On his nose sit a pair of round, antique pince-nez glasses. He doesn't need glasses, but they look the part, and that is what is important to him.

Everyone in Frankfurt who cares about books has heard of the Pilzerhoffs. That is why the tutor at the church hall near the Goethe Institute is surprised to receive Tobias's application. "Are you sure you need to join our class, Tobias? Of course, we would be delighted to have you. Only, it seems to me that a man of your credentials would be better suited to teach the class." Tobias brushes this compliment off, enjoying the recognition. "A man who stops learning stops living," he replies.

Tobias joins the creative writing group not to learn but to show off his superiority among novices, a chance seldom available within his father's literary circle. He always sits at the back to observe the attendees, sometimes scribbling notes about them, pretending to have a story in the works. None of them are writerly enough for his liking, and he does not intend to maintain any acquaintance with them.

Instead, he plans to spend the next six weeks identifying opportunities, possibly finding inspiration in the unfinished prose of others. Tobias likes to use impressive terms and jargon, dropping relevant literary terminology into his feedback. For example, if a classmate's prose includes historical elements, Tobias mentions his 'anachronistic' concerns.

He has looked forward to this evening's class since reading another attendee's submission. It is to be discussed at nine tonight, against the muted melody of the church choir practicing in the next room. Tobias readies himself, looking forward to being asked for his opinion so he can spout out the word "anaphora." When his time comes, he gives a lengthy criticism, referencing as many great literary authors as he can, pointing out any he personally knows through his father.

"Thank you for that, Tobias," says the tutor, who then moves on to another student. Tobias smiles to himself, having lost interest in the discussion, he indulges now in impressions of his own greatness. A dark-haired woman sitting behind him has been studying him intently, but he doesn't notice, so lost is he in his egotistical disorientation. Demonstrating his scholarly mastery gives him a sense of validation, strengthening his resolve that despite his lack of imagination and inability to complete a novel, one day he will, and then he can stand proud with his father.

Tobias fantasizes about such a future as he sits behind the desk, head down, pretending to read from the prose page. Nobody notices his eyes are glazed over, nor do they know that instead of being fixated on the page, his mind is glued to a vision of writing his great book. When he does sit down to write, all that comes is a hideous emptiness, followed by a tiny voice that whispers, "You are no writer, Tobias Pilzerhoff. You will never achieve what your father did." This voice drives him to evening classes, long after he has learned all the technical aspects of writing. These classes are the only place where he can drown out that voice.

He has much to prove. The praise from night classes convinces him that the energy to write his magnum opus will come. Without such praise, there is only fear.

Fear is a debilitating thing, causing writers to second-guess every word, forgetting that the basic purpose of a book is just to tell a good story. Tobias has long since forgotten this. He is focused on loftier goals, imagining himself producing a remarkable book like the one that made his father famous; the one that still affords him this privileged life.

The others in the evening class notice Tobias Pilzerhoff, though not for the reasons he imagines. They see his considered get-up, and the fact that he does not seem to be able to see through his glasses, that he seems to be reading over them. His affected tendencies stand out, eliciting eye rolls from some attendees.

Not everyone finds him irksome. Loulita Hirsch, a thin girl who also sits near the back, enjoys it when Tobias speaks out because it gives her a chance to stare openly at his sandy hair, straight nose, and aristocratic hands. She likes his jaw, which reminds her of her late father, Samuel Hirsch, as do his long legs.

After the tutor finishes handing out next week's submission, Tobias floats out the door, high on the boost to his esteem. He takes himself down by the river towards his home, recounting his triumph and forgetting, for the duration of his stroll, his writerly failings. He plans to keep up the pace and end up on top by the finish of next week's class. With plenty of time to scrutinize their efforts, he intends to come up with something cutting and clever to say. Perhaps next week he will sharpen his wit, really go to town on them, and demonstrate his merciless prowess as a literary critic.

Chapter 2

21st September 1986, Frankfurt.

"It would appear that Loulita, is it...?" Tobias glances to his right to consult the slight woman in the red jumper, who nods. "Well, you have written an... interesting piece of prose," he begins. Loulita nods, stunned to be addressed directly by the object of her scrutiny, the classmate she has been fixated on since the course began. The tutor lets out a brittle laugh. She has heard about Tobias and his cutting remarks, and hopes he does not go hard on her students. Tobias, aware of his reputation smirks, then continues.

"Here, you have chosen to highlight anaphora," he announces. "As everyone will recall, it is a device used to compound meaning through repetition. However, the sentence does not reach the arc of meaning that it might if, for example..."

A low feminine throat clearing interrupts him. Tobias turns to see Loulita with a raised hand. He pauses mid-sentence.

"I am quite sorry if you find my criticism harsh, but that is what you have signed up for..."

"Oh no," says Loulita. "It is not that at all..."

"Well, if I may continue then…?"

"It's just that…" Tobias stares. "Yes?"

"I don't think what I have written is strictly anaphora. Not precisely."

Tobias laughs. "Not anaphora?" He looks at the tutor for concurrence with a wry grin. "Is that so?" he asks, focusing on Loulita. "Perhaps you would care to elucidate what it is that you were aiming for, if not anaphora?" He glances back at the tutor with a playful wink.

"Epistrophe," says Loulita.

"What?" says Tobias, raising his brows.

"I believe it is an epistrophe."

"Loulita is correct," the tutor interjects. "Epistrophe pertains to the repetition of the same phrase or word at the end of sentences, not the beginning."

Tobias's jaw clamps up. He stares in disbelief at the woman who has just corrected him so sharply. The tutor moves on to another student. Tobias realizes they are right. How had he not seen that? The following hour feels like his head is dunked in ice-cold water. Loulita watches him, admiring his stoic restraint even in defeat. She wonders if a publisher would have noticed her own novels if she possessed even a smidgen of that stamina and poise. But no one gives her a chance. Despite being a vociferous reader and an incurable dreamer who writes exceptional stories, she cannot find anyone to take her on.

She drives a taxi, and when she speaks, it is not with the eloquent articulation of a wordsmith but with the language of humble laity. Agents and publishers fob her off. Despite her efforts, she has gotten nowhere and believes starting again is necessary. That is what brings her to the church hall near The Goethe Institute that evening.

When the class ends, she moves towards Tobias, but he waltzes past her out the door. Outside, fat pellets of rain dance off his head, and he curses the heavens for his lack of an umbrella. Lifting his leather bag to shield him, he runs towards a café across the street. There he eats two toasted ham and cheese sandwiches with pickle, then trudges towards the door, feeling nauseous.

As he crosses the street, a taxi flashes its headlights at him. The window comes down, and a timid voice says, "Tobias, do you want a lift?" It is Loulita. He walks in the pouring rain, the taxi rolling beside him. What a perfect end to the perfect day, he thinks. His stomach hurts, he is drenched, and now he is being staked out by the cause of his ire. He glances at her and back to the path.

"No, it's OK, I am fine," says Tobias, but the taxi mirrors his pace.

"You should get in..." she insists. Tobias looks at her, water trickling down his neck.

"No, it's quite OK," he says as a lorry splashes a flooded puddle at him. He shouts and pulls his saturated overcoat around him.

"You should not walk home in this rain. Now you are soaked and will be unwell tomorrow," says Loulita. Tobias huffs, then turns to the taxi, opens the door, and gets in. They sit in silence, Tobias sighing at the traffic ahead.

At a red light, Tobias puffs out at the passenger window, causing it to steam up.

"I didn't mean to, to..." Tobias looks at her. "What?"

"Back there. I was being a..." Tobias holds her stare. She blushes and shrinks down in her seat. "...a gadfly. I shouldn't have said anything, perhaps."

Tobias sighs and wipes water off his jacket sleeves. This parvenu who had humiliated him, is she now apologizing?

"Not at all," he forces himself to say. "I stand corrected." A pregnant pause follows. Loulita realizes she is giving her power away, making someone else infallible because she doesn't have the confidence to stand in her own boots and be right, even when she is right. What a cliché, she scolds herself.

14

Did she want to sleep with him? Was that it? Dr. Freud would have had a field day with her thoughts. No. She is just lonely and yearns to connect with someone of a similar mind, a desire Tobias clearly does not share. He is not like her father, only looks like him. She is trying to replace the man with phantoms.

The car stops in front of two large gates. Tobias opens the door and gets out. "Goodnight," he quips, thumping the taxi door closed. Loulita drives off, watching his silhouette in the rearview mirror. Tobias doesn't look back. Hers is not a face he will remember or care to see again. Loulita feels the same way. If only they knew that not far into the future, they would meet again through circumstances neither could have imagined.

Chapter 3

1938, Frankfurt Am Main

In Frankfurt, the August of 1938 was mild. Sunny days stretched into September, sending a leisurely wave of tanned residents towards the various city baths along the river Main for a final dip. Many went with towels and sun hats to Osthafen, or the area close to what is now the Nizza waterfront. At the river, picnic baskets brimmed with salted hard-boiled eggs, green sauce, loin ribs, Sauerkraut, Wiener schnitzels, crusty Schwarzbrot, and white cabbage coleslaw. That September, Frankfurt was the warmest city in Germany, the warmest of the larger cities at least. On average, it was two degrees hotter than Hamburg, and one degree sunnier than both Berlin and Munich. Children ran here and there in bare feet, their mouths stained pink-yellow with Bavarian onion mustard, or Düsseldorfer rote sauce. Adults sat back on blankets, fermenting in Apfelwein, and golden parental pride.

Claude Pilzerhoff was an authentic Frankfurter, a published scholar of languages, a member of the respected German elite. He liked a glass of cucumber iced water as much as the next man did, to whet his tongue on a hot September day, but other than that he didn't care much for the stuff. Water, it had the sort of illogical, nebulous property that vexed him, always got onto his papers, or seeped into the corners of his leather-bound manuscript case. And river water was by far the most disquieting. No matter how far from its banks he positioned his towel, the Main's river water wet his pen, emulsified the nib, clogging the smooth ink that rolled from its ball. Claude Pilzerhoff owned just one of those rolling ball ink pens. They were, in that year of 1938, a new invention, a pilot given to him to test by a friend called Laszlo Biro, who shortly after its creation fled to Argentina to escape what was then on its way.

Claude Pilzerhoff did not know that Laszlo's pen would someday make of his Hungarian friend a household name, or that a great calamity was about to hit Frankfurt. He only knew that when that superb pen ran out, he would have to revert to messy fountain ink. He wanted to keep it safe, away from river water, and that is why he pulled against his wife Ingrid when she cajoled and negotiated him towards the Main's fertile banks to enjoy a final dip before the Autumn fell.

Ingrid, his ten-years-younger wife, did not see things the same way as her husband did. She cared little for pens, or inventions, and saw river water in an entirely different light, so, like many women who know the makings of a good marriage, she served her husband Claude a compromise. When she managed to amputate Claude that day from whatever document he was working on, it was not by talk of the Main's river bank but with descriptions of Bad

Homburg. They took the train to that spa town north of the city where the discovery of a medicinal spring centuries ago divined in the people of Frankfurt a primal urge to be near a flowing thermal source, and from that day on brought an endless path of well-heeled feet stepping towards its southern slope, to take the air, and bathe near the Taunus mountains on warm days like this one.

Mr. Hirsch of Abraham Hirsch & Sons, Purveyor and Auction House of Rare Books and Manuscripts Frankfurt went that September day with his wife and son Samuel, to the Light and Air Baths at Volgersbrunnenweg, the only place in the city where Jewish residents were still permitted to bathe.

Claude Pilzerhoff had been employed for the past five years as a translator for Abraham Hirsch & Sons. Samuel Hirsch was Claudes age. They became acquainted at university on the tennis court. It was through this connection with Samuel Hirsch that a limitless supply of translation work rolled Claude's way. Although he felt the tightly drawn wire of malevolence that hung over the city of Frankfurt as winter approached that year of 1938, Claude Pilzerhoff could not have known that by November he, at the age of thirty-four, would be without a job, or that his employer was already planning his exile.

In the September of 1938, Claude was oblivious to the future. Despite numerous tip-offs from highly respected journalistic sources advising him otherwise, he had every intention of remaining in the city of Frankfurt, the place where he was born, baptized, educated, married and where he would die if he had his way. He could easily have left, possessed enough intelligence to have done so. He was, after all, university educated, came from a long line of other similarly educated men, and had enough understanding of Germany's undulating political landscape to have fled.

But something innate in his character stopped him from packing his few scant possessions, instructing Ingrid to do the same, emptying his safe into a neat little case, passing the keys of the third-floor apartment out of his delicate hands, and purchasing for both of them one-way first-class train tickets out of Germany.

The crux of the problem was that Claude possessed an inquisitive mind, became proportionately more interested in matters as their intensity tumefied. That is one reason why, despite acute awareness that trouble was brewing in the city, he leaned against the flow of logic, touched the air with a wet finger, and moved in the very direction of the oncoming melee. He stayed because a predisposed subcutaneous curiosity was triggered to the surface now by the commotion of the uneasy city bloating up around him. Outside his window it brewed, on the streets where he went at lunchtime to pick up a newspaper from the kiosk, or a Bratwurst from a stall.

As Jewish families hurried about Frankfurt boarding up their shops and selling off their furniture, Claude only sat back in his chair, watching, looking downward from his apartment window in fascination. He was not malicious, had no real interest in politics, did not despise Jews or anyone else. It was just that he did not ever think of getting out, not when he had documents to change from one tongue into another, when his mind was occupied by, fixated on, engrossed in his work.

Claude was detached, lived inside rigid academic preoccupation. It steadied the pen in his hand, and fixed him quite contentedly to that town of his birth. That is why under a dirigible of chaos moving slowly towards Frankfurt that Autumn, Claude sat at his desk in his quiet study inscribing a paper from French to German that discussed Goethe's theory of color as a means of psychoanalysis, and contrasted it to the ideas of an Austrian professor of neurology called Freud.

Unlike many scholars, quietness was his nemesis, the one thing that he might be depended upon to rebel against. He was ruled by some fast-moving mercurial force, was driven by the light speed mechanisms of a ticking-clock brain that worked across many plains all at once, consisted of a million moving parts, and required constant stimulation from outside himself to ward off the stale, dull heavy inertia of boredom. He worked well at home with Ingrid rustling about in the background, which is why he did not translate his manuscripts in the established chamber of the university library, where – although he knew better than to admit it – he met a dusty layer of quiet mental paralysis, one that put an end to his ability to think in two languages, two cultures, two voices at once.

From his window he could see the bright yellow hoarding over the Scala cinema at Schäfergasse, could read clearly the blazing title font of the film Holiday shining down onto passersby above the beaming airbrushed faces of Katharine Hepburn, and Cary Grant. On the stairs of his apartment in that late September of 1938, Claude Pilzerhoff met the man who rented the studio below, and felt the first personal pinch of the oncoming cloud of disruption that was by now well on its way to Frankfurt.

'Good Afternoon, Herr Pilzerhoff.' 'And to you, Herr Binderlad.'

'You have heard about the landlady already?'

'No, what about her?' said Claude

'She is gone. I witnessed her departure myself earlier today.'

'Gone? She is not staying with a friend for a night or two to escape the city?'

'With half a dozen sacks full to the brim of ornaments and vases, carrying picture frames underneath both arms?' said the man raising eyebrows above round spectacles.

'Then who will take the rent from us now?' said Claude. 'A good question,' said the man, rubbing his chin,

Binderlat chewed his inner cheek, a lozenge of consideration. Claude shrugged, tapped a foot on the parquet floor. The neighbour folded his arms, and shuffled his fingers as if to play one hand of a piano on his sleeve. Then he looked at the ceiling light fan, while Claude glanced at his watch, clearing his throat. Both sets of eyes moved fast, but they didn't meet. Neither man mentioned the nervous twitches that pulled their innards, nor the mild trapezing of their abdomens.

'Well then, if you hear anything, please do let me know, Herr Binderlat.' The next day, Claude washed his face and teeth, dressed in a neat suit, applied round spectacles similar to the ones worn by his neighbor, and took his leather satchel east along the river Main. Entering through the city gate of the Jewish quarters, the streets narrowed. When he arrived at Abraham Hirsch & Sons, he found the bookshop locked down, with no one to hand him back the thick stack of papers that sat under the counter – the rough skeleton of an academic book that he had been working on for the past year – passed over to Samuel Hirsch some weeks ago. Claude could only stare at the shut-up unit. Never before in all his time had he seen that gold and crimson metal barrier unrolled; nor the brass door frames fastened, nor the lights out, nor the ornate wrought iron pavement sign swiped in from the footpath, nor the electric menorah unlit by high noon.

In the blinking, inquisitive light of day, he peeped through the window grill for several minutes, then rapped on the door at the side for several more. After a while, he went home, and sulked in his chair.

Chapter 4

1938, November, Frankfurt

November loomed over Frankfurt like a shadowy Zeppelin, a flammable balloon that could ignite at any time with just one flit of a spark. Claude stayed in his apartment most days now reading books, chewing over the hard, bitter crust of realization that his employer – like so many other Jewish families – had gone, and that there would be no payment for the manuscript translation that had kept him here, and that his book was also irretrievable, locked in a briefcase inside Mr. Hirsch's now vacant shop. With his landlady also gone, there was no rent to pay. That was something at least. He would manage, he supposed, on his savings.

Ambling over newspaper articles – items and features that honed in on personal lives, stories and reports of ordinary people across Germany –, Claude Pilzerhoff began to notice gaping holes in the narrative; that what was written rarely reflected the reality of what he saw happening to the Jewish people on the streets around him – the ordinary man passing on his way set upon by thuggish guards with dogs, the person asked for proof of who they were, the abusive words thrown like rocks.

Claude woke in the early hours of November 9th 1938 to the sound of shouts, and of breaking glass. Peering from their bedroom window, he and Ingrid saw flares of yellow, orange flames across the city, heard the sound of night-trains rattling away for unknown destinations, smelled in their noses an infusion of smoky, burning violence, noticed troubled clouds and fires all across the medieval skyline; disturbing flashes that awakened them to the realization of the devastation spreading out from Frankfurt as far as the eye could see.

Claude ran downstairs, ran into the cityscape of charred buildings, smoking steeples, toppling infernos. He moved past broken shop windows, pushed through crowds of rioting looters – thugs with sledgehammers –, covered his mouth against the choking fumes that bellowed from broken doorways; ran towards the fires, towards the screaming, towards the sirens, towards the gates of Frankfurt's Jewish district.

Inside the cobbled ghetto, Claude turned a corner to avoid a crowd of uniformed guards slapping yellow painted stars on buildings, harassing a man against a wall. Before he got to Abraham Hirsch & Sons, Purveyor and Auction House of Rare Books and Manuscripts, he grappled a metal stick from a pile of rubble, then charged on to the street, and ran to the back of the shop. He jumped the small gate and smashed the door window into a million shards of

25

shimmering crystal. From underneath the till, he retrieved his battered brown leather briefcase. Hearing the brutish violence outside getting louder, he jumped out through the shards again, back over the fence, and darted back across town towards his apartment. Leaping through debris, rushing against the shouts, pushing bodies aside that stumbled dazed or injured in his way, he did not stop until he was behind the locked doors of his domain again.

The riots raged all night and for one more thereafter; businesses, homes, hospitals, schools, synagogues, sledgehammered to the plafonds. Hundreds died; thirty thousand Jewish men taken off to concentration camps at Dachau, Buchenwald and Katzbach; most never to be seen again. When he and Ingrid read the morning reports the next day, they could not foresee that a few days later Jews in Frankfurt would be forbidden from cinemas, theatres, operas'; that Jewish children would no longer be allowed to attend German schools.

Nazis said the new laws were made to quell Jewish uprising, hatred against the Reich, that a German diplomat in France had been shot. Whispering tongues told a different story; one not of politically motivated assassination but of a tempestuous crime of passion between an older German man and his seventeen-year old, dark-haired Jewish lover, both of whom were regulars at flamboyant Paris gay bars. It was rumored that there had been a falling out over promises made during the impatient height of lovemaking - over some murmured favor for papers of citizenship, or some other hastily made promise, retracted later - that had led to a heated row, culminating in a gunshot through the heart.

Chapter 5

1938, Frankfurt Am Main

That Christmas, Ingrid kissed Claude goodbye, and boarded a ship bound for New York to find safety with a relative. By the dawn of 1939, any New Year's Eve revelers opening sunken bleary eyes to gaze at Frankfurt would have found before them one of the last fully intact views of that medieval city. Claude himself was now holed-up in the township of his birth alone, watching from his apartment window the first hints of the awful year that was to pan out in front of him. It was thanks to the draft of the book about Frankfurt that Claude Pilzerhoff had recovered from Abraham Hirsch & Sons on Kristallnacht that our hero was able to remain in Frankfurt during 1939 and thereafter.

As the city descended into chaos, he stayed at his desk, writing to steady himself, his work granting him permission to fully escape periodically into other worlds where he could realign with his own sanity. As he continued, fragments of fiction started to occur to him, which at first he swatted away, brushing them off as early signs of dementia or psychosis. Curtly, at such times he reminded himself that he was a man of academic priority. But as the madness of war progressed, so too did the little stories that came into his mind now more and more. They assuaged his consciousness, calming certain spinning parts of his ever-moving thoughts, parts that he had failed to fully tame through crosswords, puzzles, and other disciplines up until now. It was because of these stories that one day - strictly on the condition that it was to be a jovial one-off endeavor - he humored himself into writing down one of these follies, and noticed that in doing so the gears of his creativity slipped up a notch, and began to oscillate at a faster motion than ever before. In fact, it was during that year and the ones that followed that Claude produced the best literary output of his entire career. In a heightened state of alertness - the result of living through war - a masterful story began to take shape; inspired prose made up of poignant sentences and sharp observations set against factual events. Awakened by the maelstrom, Claude's dual-powered mind cranked up a notch, and he set for himself the earnest task of painting a fictionalized picture of the war in words.

In 1940, when the RAF began to retaliate against Germany, aircraft swarmed like wasps overhead, and that was also the year that Claude began to walk the city, focusing afterwards on the pages of his book, finding now within those academic factual transcripts more and more golden opportunities for storylines that reflected real witnessed events. From then on, with every outburst of frantic engine, Claude walked the streets, his vivid accounts taking shape on paper thereafter like classic sculptures where sadness and beauty do mutually exist. That year, Claude's world became one of droning contrails, ascending and descending smoke, and the writing of beautiful fictional prose.

After 1941 rarely was there a day when Claude did not turn to his story for solace. As the skies turbined overhead, Claude sat trance-like working through some tangential detail or other. By the next year - when the RAF began its overflights, eyeing the cobbled streets, the yellow glowing wood framed taverns; attic rooms that leaned out across alleys under thatched roofs, the gothic churches, the wattle and daub houses of Sachsenhausen, the red stone walls of the Salzhaus, the heavy fortification blocks, the walls around the old city of Frankfurt Am Main - he begun editing the story. Months passed, and the disturbances became normality. Then, one day in 1942, he looked up to find a particularly dark sky, and realized that a wave of bombers was heading in. Certain that this was to be his end, he took a blanket, wrapped up in it, and shut himself in a wardrobe. When he came out, the bombardment had passed. It was thanks to bad weather over Frankfurt that day that Claude and his book survived. He got back to his work almost immediately combing through each chapter to tend to any necessary adjustments, becoming thereafter more brave, his wanderings taking him further than was wise from his home on his nightly walks.

But the lucky spell that had held Frankfurt from the worst of it was about to run out. In October 1943 devastation came in unprecedented force. It began with a distant boom, which Claude ignored as was his habit, until he felt usually strong vibrations through his chair, and witnessed his building shuffle with such force that he feared it would fall down on top of him. A low rumbling told him to move. He had just enough time to run to the basement, where he stayed for what seemed like days. When he returned to his apartment, there were cracks in the ceiling, and it was necessary to put a block under his writing desk and chair to balance them, as the floor now leaned downward so that anything left down would roll away.

Now he wore earmuffs, and a gas mask as he worked. It was in that hermetic state - one in which his breath resounded in his ears like the ocean - that he came to understand that he had created something very special, something that would be of great value to others if he could just survive. Living now for the book, Claude took less chances than he might have before. It was for the conservation of the novel - and for his

own life as its guardian - that Claude took sudden dives under his bed at the first sound of short range aircraft. Before the ornaments and bookshelves fell around him, and before the ceiling above spat dust and threatened to give way, he moved now to the basement. Cowering alone there in some dark corner, he covered the book, for he knew that within those pages were precious descriptions of his cities falling; photographic literary depictions of its skyline in various states of demise, its buildings before, after and during the worst of the attacks. He had preserved in words all that had disappeared in blinding flashes and earth-shattering booms around him. Most of Frankfurt was gone forever, but in his book it was immortalized.

Typing it up would be his next task. By February, he had passed the first blank white page into the barrel of the typewriter on his desk, and had begun documenting the book in a format that a publisher might accept. Pages became worded pictures. Out of the scraggy notepad he had been working from, a changing skyscape re-appeared, Frankfurt reimagined in tapping strikes of an inked ribbon. By March, the stack of paper had grown to some height. Against the backdrop of the research conducted for his original text, a city in the tenebrous flux of war took shape which included heartbreaking fictionalized human stories. By the summer, the story was a readable first-hand sketch of bombs and destruction, of human reality, of survival, and loss. His words amounted to a story as unsettling, and factual as the torn faces of Hepburn and Grant, who watched in a faded stupor from the opposing cinema façade.

As troubled rumblings strained Frankfurt into siege; as the largest medieval German metropolis buckled under ten thousand tons of explosives, Claude Pilzerhoff typed up his draft. Then he left his fortress to stroll amongst the ruins just as he had been doing for years, counting the fallen churches, stopping here and there outside the gravelly piles of the timber-framed houses that had come down during the night, – events witnessed by devastated inhabitants and standers- by. He was used to noting the weather, how the rain had felt, the smells and sounds, what shoes people living through those shocking times chose to wear on their feet, and he was used to keeping low key as he passed the guards but making sure to gather details of them just the same, because it was on such factual particulars that his book was built.

During the early years of the war, the SA guards had questioned Claude Pilzerhoff, pushing him up against a wall, not letting him pass, but that did not stop him coming out the next night to walk amongst new mountains of smoking debris, or the next one to investigate what damage last night's thunderous explosions had whistled downward all around while the cities remaining inhabitants had lain in their trembling beds. The soldiers didn't bother him much anymore. Instead, they only shook their heads or told him to go away, advising him that it was dangerous. As time went on, they came to ignore him altogether, turning a blind eye as one might disregard a madman, a person too insane to argue with. Now if they did interfere with him, it was only to throw their eyes to heaven as he went by, or to make some silly gesture. One soldier always bleated like a goat. Another made circular motions with their fingers about Claude to their comrade to indicate that he was not right n the head. Only the odd one laughed at him because everyone knew him. And he knew them too.

He knew they called him The Baker of Bornhein, the man who counted reducing buildings as a cook might watch over a reducing soup, or a stack of Brötchen. Most of the soldiers were young men, some he estimated still in their teens, terrified country boys far from home, and way out of their depth. Claude didn't ask questions. And none of the Guards ever mentioned the trains or talked about where those new tracks ended. He heard whispers, counted what he could capture with his eyes and wrote it down later; the five and a half thousand bodies lost to the bombings. He counted the carriages that barreled in empty and left full, made estimations based on their capacity. He counted those Jewish people who were pulled out, beaten, taken away and who never returned during the torturous years that annexed the destruction of Frankfurt am Main. As the lunatic times rolled on, Claude lost the politeness that defines society.

It happened slowly so that he hardly noticed. It was sometime around 1940, when France was occupied by

Germany that there came through Frankfurt a stream of French accents, passing through Frankfurt's train station on their way to Switzerland. Dazed from the long train journey, and in need of a smoke, a man had wandered out of the train-station in a blind fugue of disorientation, and staggered muzzy-headed right into Claude on the street.

'Can you tell me if there is a clock nearby?' said the man, revealing an unfamiliar lilt. 'I wish to check these new eye-glasses to ensure I can see properly with them.' Claude, with the remnants of common politeness still intact pointed at an old bank across the street. 'Look up at the roof there. The clock is still keeping time, I believe,' he said. The man looked up blinking at the broken clock.

'I can't see it,' he said. Not knowing quite what to say, feeling then uncomfortable to be talking to another human about matters that once defined civil communication, Claude became harried, and fearful of being inveigled into the madness of another persons trauma. And Claude said something then which he would never forget; something a man of his academic background would never have said prior to the war. It was just after the sentence had left his mouth that he vowed never to converse with a stranger in such circumstances again. 'If you imagine it's there, you might see it."

At these words, the man peered, and squinted towards the building and the clock so clearly inoperable, and Claude excused himself, projecting his legs past the stranger as fast as they would go. ' I still can't see it,' said the man to nobody, staring, abandoned, looking bewildered up at a smashed clock face.

During the years that followed, Claude rarely encountered another soul and crossed the footpath if he did. Mainly, he watched and wrote until one chilly night late in the summer of 1944 an armed soldier bounded towards him, stepping hard against the cobbled street so that Claude thought he might then be shot by an assassin running high on the propaganda of hatred.

'You are a translator?' asked the soldier. 'Yes, I am.'

'You know Yiddish?'

'I am German,' demanded Claude.

'You can read Jewish writing?' said the soldier again.

'I am a scholar of languages. Hebrew is one of them,' said Claude, aware that lesser offences had seen men thrown into a train. At the verification of his credentials, the soldier said nothing more, but instead pushed a greasy package at Claudes chest. He instinctively closed his arms around it.

'What is this?' asked Claude, looking down at the contents of his hands.

'It's a story.' said the soldier.

'Where did you get it?' But the soldier only blinked, then averted his eyes, confirming in quietness all there was to say about the source. Claude watched as the soldier retreated, a moving phantom engulfed by the darkness of a smoking cobbled street. A shadow, then nothing. Raising the package to his nose, the stench hit him, causing him to jolt away. It stunk of engine oil, of sweat and onions, and all manner of greasy hideousness. He might have opened it there and then, only something about that ominous package seemed too sacred to disturb on the bare street outside. So he pushed it inside his coat, and moved on fast towards his home. Despite his cool, detached exterior, and the jamming stabs of curiosity that came as he carried it under his arm; by the time he laid it on the table of his apartment and touched the twisted twine with a shaking hand, he drew away, sensing that in opening it, he would be creaking the lid off a vast chest of sorrow. He did not want to uncover such a thing, not alone, not within this time of chaos, not when he didn't know if he would survive from one day to the next. Certain that it came from the place at the end of those train tracks to nowhere, that package needed time. It would be put away, he decided, until he was ready, until his current project was fulfilled.

And so he left that package still wrapped in the greasy cloth that smelled of onions and sweat, of chamber pots and unwashed clothes, of train oil and rotting teeth, of disease and blood, out of sight; put it away in a special place, in a rarely used compartment in his bureau. He slipped it into that slim little panel separate from the other drawers so that he wouldn't see it, and wouldn't smell it when he went looking for a page, or ink or typewriter ribbon. Then he continued with his other writing until he forgot about it amongst the chaos that came with every new day, distracted by his work, by war, and by the preoccupation that defined him.

Chapter 6

March, 1945, Frankfurt

On the last day of March 1945, Claude Pilzerhoff woke to the sound of American voices.

'I love you, Katharine Hepburn,' one man shouted from outside the Scala cinema, standing in front of the torn poster, his arms outstretched.

'You are free, Princess,' said another, blowing kisses at the by now distressed hoarding.

'Time to go home,' said the third.

Claude looked down and saw, on the street below, tanks with white stars, moving slowly between multitudinous olive troops, waving red, white and blue flags. 'Frankfurt, you are free,' they shouted up at the surrounding edifices, but Claude only ducked behind his curtain, too afraid to believe what seemed like the end. People came running out onto the streets, those who had survived. Soldiers picked up children, swung them around, their blackened faces paraded in victory through the streets. By April 1945, Frankfurt was in the control of the Allied forces. Although he heard the news straight from the young American soldiers who inundated the streets, pushing their guns through rubbish for survivors, Claude was not convinced that a ceaseless war machine would not push a sinuous rotting hand up from the grave and fire up its reign of evil terror once again.

September brought news of the Führers suicide in a bunker in Berlin. It was confirmed. The war had ended. Laszlo Biro, Claude's friend in Argentina, wrote him a note saying that he planned to begin mass production of those ball point pens. In the note he suggested he could send a few more to Frankfurt, but Claude did not receive the note because he had already turned his observations and writings into a book, and had left Frankfurt for the USA.

For the next few years, Claude Pilzerhoff travelled around those fifty states, talking in front of large groups of people. It was in those years that he became known as the voice of hope. The people who came to listen came not because they cared about literature, but because they had no other place to put their tears, no graves for the ones who had disappeared, no knowledge of how it had been for them, of what had happened to them during those severed years. The words that Claude had written from 1939 to 1945 - the ones that made up his book, the accounts that he spoke of in front of the crowds - allowed them to know, gave them a place to put their grief, enabled them to fill in the voids left by the unanswered letters they had sent across the Atlantic during and after the war. For many, Claude Pilzerhoffs book was the only answer they ever received, the only news of the loved one who had been ripped from them; of the living turned into nothingness, of looming grief, and unanswered questions, historical accounts of a crumbling city alongside human stories. It was comfort in the deadly quietness of lost memories, unsaid 'goodbyes', a buffer for loss, a substance for people to place their sorrows into, to put endings to the lives that they had abandoned. Though it did not describe exactly what had happened at the end of the train tracks, it did describe the bombed buildings, shootings and murders. The unaccounted-for millions were not treated just as facts and figures for a historical log, but as people who the readers knew as someone's uncle, father, grandfather, son, sister, or mother; people who had been taken from them without an ending.

In 1959, Claude Pilzerhoff reunited with his wife Ingrid in New York, and in December of 1960, when Claude was 56 and she 46, a child was born, a little boy called Tobias.

Chapter 7

March, 1988, Frankfurt,

The Spring of 1988 brought news that Claude Pilzerhoff had died after a short battle with pancreatic cancer. Particulars regarding his beloved father's remains crashed against the drifting detachment of Tobias's grief. Kept afloat by means which he did not accredit to his own strength, Pilzerhoff Junior felt his head nodding at the word 'cremation', saw his finger extending toward a photograph of an urn in a catalogue at a funeral home, then watched the same digit slide over the page to land on a gravestone.

At some point, he heard himself say, 'yellow roses.' When Probate and Will were mentioned, his countenance assumed the correct position, one that mimicked that of a listening man, and when it was time to scratch his name onto a cheque to cover the cost of these customary expectations, he complied with the same composure and mute solemnity.

After the funeral, Tobias strode down the gravelly cemetery path, and walked out the gate. A few minutes later, he came to the path that ran along the river Main. Walking through unsympathetic rain showers, a bewailing wind blew callous leaves into his face, a cyclist splashed by soaking his feet with puddle water, as drunken revelers on riverboats jeered past. He went by museums, crossed several bridges, and at last came to a stop in front of a street corner window, at a junction near the Altstadt; a real estate shopfront, where his eyes fixated on a Perspex enshrouded photograph of a Bavarian palace.

Throbbing grief rose up in Tobias's esophagus at the sight of its fairy-tale turrets, and the water that encircled it; details that stirred up the summer plans that he and his father had made for Bavaria: They had meant to go on a hiking expedition to the mountains, traipsing by day between its thirty-two Ludwigian Schlösser, visiting each one in turn, pitching a tent for the night on a grassy pasture nearby to look back at each splendiferous jewel lit up against its own unique backdrop; at the panorama of rolling white capped alpine peaks, or endless green, needled forest, their lungs filled with clean air, the fresh aroma of spruce saplings vacillating at their noses and crackling pork spitting from a fire.

Tobias had walked behind his father in every aspect of his life, including his academic pursuits. Like Claude, he had studied English, French and Hebrew at Frankfurt's Goethe-Universität, and he had hoped one day to see the glow of pride on his father's face when he too would write a great book that would captivate hearts. Now that would never happen, and those castles would remain a poetic fantasy, a lost dream for some other father and son to enjoy. Tobias looked at the address written underneath the photograph. Düsseldorf it said.

Following his father's death, Tobias Pilzerhoff took over his father's contacts. He translated academic documents, made a living, wrote plays, was celebrated and embraced by the Frankfurt literary community, but knew deep down that the welcoming hand of his contemporaries - the silver- tongued projections of editors and agents, the invitation, the opportunities - only came his way because of his father's work, because of Claude Pilzerhoffs writing; because the old mans books had received awards, were held up, commended for their contribution to history, culture and humanity. Tobias's first book came out the same spring that his father passed, tied to the clattering noisy hype and anticipation that the son would do with a pen what the father had.

Wilhelm, his silver-foxed agent, pushed the book into shops on the back of the father's funeral, launched it the same week, at the very time when news of the older man's departure was making headlines all over the world, that the notable passing of the words of a man who had filled in the void of nothingness for so many people after the war would inspire the nation to loosen their wallets a second time for the son's contribution to literature.

Critics were kind about Tobias's novel, left out what they didn't need to say, or castigated the work only between the lines. They were sparing in their directness, veered towards uplifting language, vague praise, but in terms of sales – the true barometer, the proof of a book's commercial value, of whether people actually cared about its content, whether they were truly affected by the story enough to keep turning its pages until the end – of those there were only a handful, not even ten thousand copies sold.

The agent had made as good a job of promoting that book as was possible with the meagre scrapings that it offered. As predicted, the group who did buy the son's book were made up mostly of those who had been affected by the father's work. They bought the sons book in the hope of finding something of the father's powerful transcendence, but in vain. Tobias's book was devoid of his fathers creative flair. It contained no trace of the staggering prose, not the delicate observations that caused wells of emotions to break through and fall from the eye, not the pictures in painted words that soothed and salved the heart after tears had fallen.

Nonetheless, for Tobias Pilzerhoff that summer was a haze of publicity, of radio interviews, of TV appearances and of shaking hands with journalists. Tobias enjoyed several nights out in the front row amongst the theatre set of Frankfurt, the flirtations of coat-tale grasping starlets, some kind speeches in his honor, ones that invariably linked him back to his father in the end. People patted his back, raised glasses of champagne to his new book, asked him to attend signings, and requested that he speak. He received some hampers of fruit, Camembert and Riesling, but no real acclaim or recognition outside of Germany or even Frankfurt.

Winter set in, and the thin layer of self-delusion that Tobias had been standing upon about his writing began to wear thin. On the eve of his thirtieth year, he sat down at his father's writing desk, in the very position that his father had assumed when ideas had flown to him; his elbows on the table, his hands in clasped meditation, and prayed for some nebulous hand of divine inspiration to come down from the heavens and touch him. But it didn't. Night after night, Tobias closed his eyes, sat in silence in that same position before the word processor like an obedient pupil in a tweed smoking jacket with leather patches on the elbows. But still nothing came.

He lit Nag Champa incense, burned stimulating oils, took baths with crystal amulets, underwent fasting procedures so that hunger might make room for the invigoration of imagination. A calmness came over him, a pleasant feeling, one that helped him sleep better, but it did not bring on even the flutter of an idea of brilliance, no such glimmer of inspiration, no concept that could be harnessed, and developed into a novel sturdy enough to stand proud and walk in the literary footsteps of his father.

In September, Ingrid went back to New York, sold the family home. Tobias retreated to the hills outside Frankfurt, had the old man's writing desk, and books installed in his study. But still no flash of eureka came.

Chapter 8

November, 1988, Frankfurt

November trudged in like a lonesome ice-hiker, crushing more thuds of heavy booted self-doubt down on Tobias's morale. For his thirtieth birthday, Tobias did not take himself off on holiday to The Villa Rothschild to christen the day with a cool bottle from the deep wine cellar, or lose himself in the chilled giggling bubbles of a glass of Brut. Not one single cut flute of sparkling Sekt passed his lips. Neither did he go to the Steigenberger Frankfurter Hof hotel as he had with his father so many times before to convalesce, to sleep in a soft bed and soothe his neck on a puffed-out feather-filled Egyptian cotton pillow, nor did he book a table in a restaurant to dine with friends before the Rhein-Main; no graceful speech in advance of haute cuisine, no slither of rare blue mignon to commend the years that he had been alive. Not one luxury item did he purchase for himself to mark three decades; not some finely crafted shiny leather shoes, nor a cheerful winter scarf. Not one word of self- praise did he allow into his mind, not even modest alms of kudos, nor one sneaky uplifting self-compliment. He only served to his psyche that day a harsh plate of self-criticism, quiet head-shaking dismay at his creative inadequacy and failings as a writer, and as a son.

Taking a walk in the city park that morning, his eyes did not dance at the sight of pine trees sprinkled white with snow, did not stop to gaze in wonder at the white swans that sprayed the lake water, their flailing angelic wings fluttering in celebration of the crystallizing beauty of a winter's dawn. Because he knew nothing of the arrival of the luck-changing avalanche that was rolling towards him. That evening, he did the very same thing that he had done each night for years. Unaware that a bounty was about to fall into his lap, he pressed the ON button of the word processor and watched the screen illuminate, eyes fixed on the cursor winking its Morse code of nothingness, as it had done so many times before. With a shuffle of irritation, he huffed, scowled, furrowed his brow, folded his legs, and moved his defeated thighs under the desk, reefing the plug socket out as he did, cutting the power to the computer, causing the screen to go black, closing the eye of that blinking cursor.

Crouched down under the table to fix the problem, whilst shuffling with the cable to re-insert the plug, he placed, quite by accident, his hand underneath his father's desk and fondled something odd, an uneven piece of wood. He patted it several times before putting his face up close to the previously unseen compartment beneath the bureau. There he noticed a slither of yellow metal, the thin brass handle of a hidden drawer. A sharp yank yielded nothing. Then,

49

jostling the stiff swollen wood on the underside of the desk, he forced the slim drawer open with his pen and pulled from it a crinkled aged parcel, the same one a faceless German soldier had passed to his father, the translator Claude Pilzerhoff, all those years ago on a dark street in Frankfurt.

Tobias placed the package on the desk before him, looked back into the drawer, then turned the wrapped-up item over. There was no note to indicate the parcel's origins, no university or book vendor's stamp, no instruction. He picked it up and sniffed the wrapping paper. By now, the foreboding stench that had warded his father off had mellowed, was just a trace of something old – soggy, rotten cabbage, or moss from a distant stagnating pond, perhaps. He pulled the rope twine, picked the knot that held it together, and pushed the crisp hardened brown paper wrapping away.

Before him now, on his father's old desk, lay a russet colored hardback notebook, thread binding dry, the paper yellowed, neat angular lines, patterns of a three-thousand year-old language, one he knew well, had studied at university. Eyeballs moving over the pages of familiar icons - Chets, Shins and Tavs - he picked up the introductory lines of a handwritten story, a carefully transcribed novel penciled in the Hebrew alphabet. Tobias Pilzerhoff read on, and learned that the author had turned thirteen in the winter of 1941, within the packed confines of a death camp at

50

Katzbach outside Frankfurt, and that she had written down this story in Yiddish so that no German soldier would ever know what it said.

The first paragraph revealed how it had never occurred to her that even a healthy young body like her own could smell worse than a putrescent corpse; that the stench of sweat could become more offensive than fermenting turnips, that armpits could pong like moldy bread, feet smell worse than foul blue cheese, and that an ordinary scalp and strands of hair could absorb the stink of all these things combined, to become a noxious, odoriferous greasy sponge more rancid than dishwater steeped in rotten oily fish, when deprived for just one month of water, soap and the cleansing warmth of sunlight.

There was, he learned, for the author of that manuscript, no escape from the odious deterioration of her body, or from that of the thousands of others around her. She wrote amongst people, dozens of people, all crammed together, their final months spent in hairs-breath proximity to each other - in a place where a horrific black cloud, a putrescent fog of death, hung thick in the air overhead. Under the corrugated roof of a crowded shed, huddled night after night, waiting to die, she wrote. He learned that the book had come out of a malignant time in history, a time when the tumorous decay of human cruelty proliferated and stunk like rotten eggs and sour milk. The author, a young girl, was a prisoner sentenced to die like all the rest. The story in his possession had been penned in dwindling light as divisive darkness and ignorance mutated and spread with every new day outward from Germany to Poland, oozing and pulsating then on to Finland, Denmark, Norway, Luxembourg, the Netherlands, Italy, The Soviet Union, to Romania, Hungary, Bulgaria, and Greece.

Trapped inside that murderous pit of skeletal bodies, she wrote amongst the dying, dead, maimed, and diseased, where young and old lay together in scurvied ragged piles, in endless rows, breathing smoke from the burning pyres of those already discarded; in a place of lice infested skin and shaven heads, of open sewage, of choking sulfurous toxic fumes, the reek of desolation. Waiting for death in that charnel house, a last longing came over that girl, to fill her lungs just one last time with something sweet and pure and clean. So intensely had she willed herself to taste the goodness of life again, to detach all senses - from the sickening fugue of ugly intolerance, and boarded-up hearts, from the sound of incessant innards functioning the biological workings of a thousand guts around her; the rumbling gaseous secretions of miles of intestines, the gurgling acid rot of starving bellies, from the moans, the snores, the rancid stench of decaying teeth, the mucus filled lungs - and worst of all from the contagious, awful funk of dwindling hope and of broken spirits. Only she could not.

Her last chance of escape from that revolting crematorium of death would only come through the projections of the mind. And so she set about creating a different world. That is why, when, on her thirteenth birthday, that girl pulled the book now laid out on Claude Pilzerhoffs old writing desk, and a pencil from the stiff hands of a rigor mortised corpse, she wrote not about the horrors surrounding her, but instead, she wrote about the beauty of life.

In scripted Hebrew, there came from that young soul a fragrant picture of a longed-for world; of grassy hills, and sticky alpine cones, of white jasmine twilight blooms, of baking doughnuts, of lush flower blossoms, of roasting Christmas chestnuts, and playing children in lavender Spring meadows, biscuity puppies snoring sound, of fruit orchards lush and sweet, and serried beds of candy roses, pink floral carpeted hills, the makings of a cerebral scent, one so pure, so refined, so gentle - a cherubs perfume fit for heaven itself.

Down wandered Tobias Pilzerhoff 's eyes through sentences of sweet-smelling bouquets, of chocolate's pleasures, an olfactory garden of delicate colored swirling beauty, of golden ylang ylang; the projections of sensory longing, a poetic wall of celestial defence, a boundary between that writer and her awful reality. Against the rot of hate, she cast with words a protective cloak, a story of natures truth, of the rules of the earth, innocent evocations, visions of magnificent splendor, a universal intelligence, or whatever it is that causes hearts and minds to shift, and change, and transmute and move upward; to forget conceit, and about being right, but instead to soften and mellow, and form themselves unyielding into joyful vessels of harmonious love.

More than a quarter of a century before Tobias Pilzerhoff was born, a forgotten hand had filled that notebook with such. Now the son of Claude Pilzerhoff - who had lived, and wrote his way through a war, who had given hope to so many with his words when it ended - had found that story. Tobias scratched his chin, examined his thoughts one last time to check if, by the chance in a million, the Gods had chosen this same moment to send that elusive grain of inspiration his way. On finding nothing, Tobias Pilzerhoff began that very night translating the first paragraphs from Yiddish to German at his father's desk; a story not his own, but one that would be read by twenty-five million people in fifty different languages, and make of him, in just a few short years the most famous writer in the world.

Of course, Pilzerhoff knew none of this, nor was he particularly taken with that story. Being the man he was, he was affected by the linguistic engineering of the piece,

the exposition and semantic architecture, on getting the equivalent terminology right verbatim. Yiddish is a German dialect which uses many Hebrew words, and so he was well equipped for the job. A practical goal appeared before him, and his mind fixed on translating that novel with clarity, accuracy, conciseness, and proper order of adaptation. These being areas in which Tobias Pilzerhoff excelled, he applied the full force of himself to them, and lost all thought of the person behind the words.

He would not have taken to the task at all, or paid much notice to that ragged book, but for one prevailing fact, without which, that locked drawer would have remained so, and that story would still be there today. Only it isn't, because Tobias found himself at that moment, once again idle, devoid of inspiration, lacking personal creativity, and with absolutely nothing else to write.

Such were the arbitrary forces that came together on that winters evening, which led Tobias Pilzerhoff to open a new file on his word processor, create a folder named The Scent of Heaven, and dedicate himself wholly to translating the book that had appeared quite by chance before him.

Chapter 9

June, 1989, Frankfurt

As Frankfurters walked amid the rolling carpet hills of the Taunus picking fragrant summer herbs for yogurt green sauce with cold potato salad, Tobias Pilzerhoff posted a story to Berlin. Wilhelm, his agent, greeted the news of the new novel with skilful diplomatic guile.

'So soon?' he smiled down the phone, restraining the belching reflux that the prospect of another groaning publicity-run with Tobias's literary efforts was already costing his digestive system. Opening the envelope containing Tobias's new book, he rubbed his stomach at the thought of the upcoming efforts necessary to extract winning testimonials, the conveyor belt of cheese and wine hampers that would be required, the multitudinous kindly worded letters paper-clipped to early editions that would be vital to achieve at least one or two snappy quotes of praise. Such was the work now facing him, work that would be needed to produce the favorable front-cover recommendations essential to sell the book, and make a sizable dint on a print- run; a sales dint steep enough to ensure Tobias's confidence in him and so retain the lucrative publishing entitlement of the father's work, the royalties of which made up the lifeblood of his publishing house.

Popping a pepper-mint into his mouth for steely enthusiasm and to settle his tummy, Wilhelm rolled up his sleeves, brought the manuscript into his sitting room, clenched his jaw, turned his eyes to the task at hand, sat down rigid backed on his sofa and ordered himself to focus; to wade through the meandering, overgrown tangle of weedy prose, the eye-drooping choke, the wandering narrative maze that he expected to find within that vault of words.

He needn't have worried. It wasn't so bad. Fact was, it could even be described as palatable. No, it was better than that. Way better. His eyes roamed the sentences, moved across the pages and back, taking in words, unexpected ones, combinations that brought vivid beautiful pictures to his mind, heavenly sentences, so finely selected, so crisp and ripe with purity; sensate descriptions of sweet-smelling gardens, of divinity so tasteful that it caused him almost to forget to breathe. At one point, and quite without meaning to, Wilhelm came closer and closer to the page until it was right up to his nose, his skin touching the manuscript. Almost running out of breath, he caught himself panting. So he stopped, took to shaking his head, to rubbing his eyes and blinking.

Then, he read on. But on taking in more of Tobias's story, his senses capitulated, became seduced once more by the fusion of words that spritzed toward him from the page in a delicate veil of lush fragrant dewy grassy passages. He started again and the same thing happened once more.

It was a dancing stream of intoxicating, irresistible poetry, a resinous story that clung to the perception, more provocative and alluring than anything he had ever read before. Closing his eyes, he allowed himself to take a moment, to regain a hold, before one more paragraph. Only he reverted quite naturally back to the same stance. Savoring the impressions within the story, he sailed away, letting himself go this time, enticed down lanes of Jasmine gardens, poemy and meadows of rose, lavender and bergamot, drifting off on a wave of peaceful hypnosis to some long-forgotten memory; a vision of his former self, as a youthful man, then him as a boy frolicking through a woody glade of honey suckled musical chords. He felt something at his leg, and a warmth by his hand. It was his childhood friend Harold, come back to life, his companion for a decade. Stooping down, he picked up the wriggling ball of warmth, rolled amongst the flowers enshrouded in glorious floral hugs, and wet dog kisses. He laughed, writhing about the floor of his sitting room, the paragraphs caressing every part of his fondest memories, playing a captivating melody on each of his faculties all at once, so crystalline and majestic that he cried a tear of involuntary pleasure.

With that single drop of water that fell from his cheek, every crease of anguish, every line of worry left his face, until in a drowsy, stupefied daze of exhilaration, he put Tobias's manuscript down, let his arms flail at his sides, stretched out on the floor and, with a blissful smile spread across his face, felt his entire body soften. Then he melted back. Doe-eyed with contentment, he dozed as if drunk on frothy herbaceous elderflower beer, strawberry wine, or garden apple cider, and slept then more peacefully and subdued than he had in all his conceivable adult life.

Chapter 10

October 1989, Berlin

That October, a landslide of revellers descended upon Berlin. Some stripped naked in the streets, frolicked in the cities drinking fountains. Others cried tears of pent-up joyful sorrow, dug bare fists into the crumbling stony gravel of the falling wall, tearing apart the divisive blocks that had for almost three decades coldly split East and West Germany.

The crowd was made up of young and old, rich and poor, and every socio-economic, geographic, political milieu in between. In the mix that flowed into the German capital that Summer, that Summer, were droves of movie stars and celebrities, Kings and Barons, poets, socialites, painters, fashion designers, models, producers, journalists and an endless white champagne tent entourage of the impossibly beautiful people that accompanied them around the globe.

To the countryside came a bustle of colorful visitors who parked up in disused fields, set up tents and strung lights with generators. They were mostly travelers, gypsies and free-spirits, posh punks with fancy accents on the run from Thatcherism, or university drop-outs, rebels, and middle-aged hippies from all parts of Europe and beyond. They danced and mingled to beats and base, swam in a sea of drumming and diversity. Some called themselves 'ravers', others preferred 'techno head' all knew the name C-8, the lead singer of The Stoics.

In the city center, five bare-chested men stood on top of the fractured wall, sledgehammering sections of it away, whilst C-8 stood scratching his stubbly chin, facing a television camera as someone clipped a wire to his shirt. Exhaling a reefer from the side of his mouth, he flipped a dangerous cloak of dark purple hair, revealing outlined raven eyes. A yellow, spongy microphone came forward, someone shouted 'rolling', and Europe's breakthrough singer lit up with the charisma that had made him a star.

Smooth and cheerful, he listened thoughtfully, then answered questions about his dissident performances, about the group's skyrocketing global success, the track that had swallowed up more sales in a week than most did in a lifetime. He talked for the first time on global television about the melody and its lyrics, the anthem for social reform, democracy and freedom at the site of the reunification of Berlin, and on why he thought that tune was whizzing its melodic orbit around the planet.

'What inspires you during the songwriting process?' the gushing bleachy-headed interviewer asked.

61

'I don't know. Just life, I suppose. Reading, maybe.' 'Any book in particular that you can think of?'

'Yes, there is one. It only came out in the summer, but I've read it about five times already. I've got it right here,' said the singer, pulling a dog-eared damson cover from his pocket.

'The Scent of Heaven by Tobias Pilzerhoff,' said the interviewer. 'I've heard of it. What do you like so much about that book?'

'I don't know. It calms me. If I have anxiety before a show, I'll take it out and read it.'

'What is it about?'

'A young girl who walks through rose gardens searching for the nectar of life. She goes on a trip to find the most perfect smell, down a riverboat of flowers.'

'Sounds intense.'

'It's living, breathing poetry. This book has a depth and richness unlike anything I have ever read before. So much feeling. It makes me cry, and I can't explain why.'

'Have you ever used books as inspiration for any of your songs?'

'I never did before, but this story got me here,' he said a fisted thump to his heart. 'As a matter of fact, I used it to write our latest release.'

'You mean "Sweet City"?'

'That's the first time I've ever done it, but yes, Sweet City is based on that little girl and her floral episodes.'

'It must be a pretty special kind of story,' said the interviewer.

'Can't say I've read anything so beautiful before. I carry that book with me everywhere I go. See?' said the singer returning the book to the breast pocket of his shirt.

With the TVs volume turned down, a Russian man slumped on the bed of a Dresden hotel room, and supposed he would return to St. Petersburg now. What was there for a KGB agent to do in East Berlin now? He was among the millions of people who tuned into the Stoic's MTV broadcast that day. A week later, not one single copy of The Scent of Heaven was left in any bookshop in Germany. Word spread. It was not long before printing presses heaved to keep up with the demand as a crew of translators sweated through manuscripts in their respective countries.

The Portuguese were the first to hand their translation over to their local publishing house, followed closely by the French. The English edition came out next, the Japanese shortly before the Chinese, whose translators had received their instructions late, because deliberating authorities had withheld the contents of the book for almost three days. The color red had caused a problem. It was described in so many different ways that agents thought it could be a code. An elite squad of intelligence officers were dispatched to check for hidden ciphers in the text. These rumors when leaked by Wilhelm only made buyers more curious about the book, only proliferated demand. When Beijing were finally able to start working on their translation, Wilhelm plagued the international publisher's head of house from Berlin on the hour to check for updates, harrying the team of translators to confirm when the first batch of books would arrive in shops so that he would not be accountable for an international situation caused by the tents of young people who were now obstructing footpaths outside every major city bookshop in the Chinese capital.

By the summer, the subversive London fashion designer George King had been photographed leaving a restaurant with a copy under his arm. Shortly after, the designer sent catwalks into a frenzy of theatrical performance, his creations heavily influenced by the floral scenes of that years international best-selling novel. The front-row fashion editors, who had watched the launch show in restrained awe, described it as a seductive journey into a fabric paradise. Models in layered silk dresses dangled crimson, cherry, burgundy, dark velvet and auburn from silken ropes of vine adhered to the ceiling, and at one point during the show, a cascade of one million petals rained down on top of the crowd.

In Paris, the fragrance director at Dior released, to great applause, a new scent, one built on olfactory notes inspired by The Scent of Heaven. It arrived in department stores, was stacked high in shiny, irresistible poppy red ruby encrusted triangles that diminished almost as fast as they could be replenished. By Christmas, every shop window on the Champs-Élysées was illuminated with flowers, the Eiffel Tower lit red underneath a huge flashing scarlet rose.

More marriage proposals were recorded that year than in the previous five, and of that fecund procession of brides, the most fashionable ditched the virginal white vestments that sang of purity and innocence to stride the aisles of Paris, Berlin, New York and London in scandalous, audacious, unrestrained desirous shades of ruby, crimson, chili pepper, black cherry, even daring polka-dot ladybird satin with lips to match.

In Indonesia and Mumbai, batik cloth producers – the ones who supplied wedding dress fabrics to the world's fashion houses – switched back to traditional dying methods, ancient techniques not seen for centuries, in which forgotten sources of pigment were distilled: bark, berries, even insects were crushed into paste, boiled and soaked to stain textiles when synthetic processes could no longer meet the insatiable demand for the hypnotic allure of rambunctious, unapologetic red fabric of a world-wide incursion of floral romance that had come from a book.

Chapter 11

January, 1990, Berlin

In January, the first sprinkling of royalties fell upon Tobias Pilzerhoff, and a blizzard of interview requests snowed

up the letter-box of Wilhelm.

'Jeffrey Stein here, from The Times of New York City.' 'Hello Jeffrey,' said Wilhelm, his long bulbous nose sniffing out the extent of the other man's offering all the way across the Atlantic.

'Can you get Tobias over here for an interview next week?'

'Well, I don't know, Jeffrey. He doesn't like flying, cramped airplanes and all that.'

'We will take him first class, then.' 'That might work,' said Tobias's agent.

'You have a fine eye for scouting writers, Wilhelm.'

'Oh, I saw the potential in Tobias ever since he was a small boy, indeed it was I who gently pushed him into the craft,' said Wilhelm.

'We look forward to meeting him. What are the exact sales figures of The Scent of Heaven now?

'We just came over one million copies this week.'

'A fine accomplishment. Hats off to you for your part in it.'

'Yes, a lot of work. I am utterly exhausted, could do with a holiday?'

'I can imagine,' said Jeffrey. Wilhelm let the conversation breath before taking it up again. 'Normally, a small something is thrown in for my efforts, if you know what I mean. Arranging a transatlantic interview with an artiste of such delicate sensibilities is no mean feat. After all, Tobias only agrees to talk to people that I recommend.'

'I see.'

'It's just that my wife Cynthia has always wanted to see the Statue of Liberty in the snow…'

'Consider it done,' said the editor.

'…and to enjoy the view of Central Park from a hotel window?'

'The Ritz Carlton is near there. That will suffice?'

'…and a car at the airport so that Tobias does not get cold?'

'A driver will take all three of you.'

'Oh, and some flowers in the room. Roses for Cynthia.'

'OK.'

'Tobias enjoys the light, buttery air of orchids.'

'Sure.' In New York, Jeffrey scratched his chin, leaving the agreement to marinade.

'So that's it then. It is arranged?'

'White orchids, if that is not too much trouble. He does love flowers.'

'OK.'

Tobias arrived at Wilhelm and Cynthia's home in Berlin that night, where his agent greeted him at the door in stocking feet.

'You.' He waggled a finger at Tobias, then grabbed his upper arms, shaking him.

'You. You. You,' said Wilhelm, sending Merlot fumes into Tobias's face.

'YOU!' he added with a side-eyed beam, showing his protégé a full set of tannin-stained teeth.

'You've done it,' he said, taking the liberty of giving his client a bear-hug, and rocking him back and forth in his arms. 'Why didn't you tell me that you were working on your magnum opus?' he slurred into the neck of the man he had cast off as a three-legged donkey, as a non-runner, as the dwelt of the stable: never thinking this one had it in him to outrun the rest, end up the winner that brought home the trophy, the man who - without even a dollop of publicity, without even one single, laborious trudge around the racecourse of press, without any over-zealous hyped up compliments down the phone to doubting critics - had sold more in a few months than any of his other publishing punts had in a decade.

'It's the big one, Tobi' he said, sweeping snow from Tobias's epaulettes, and ushering him into the sitting room. 'The Times of New York City, my good man,' he said, chest out leading Tobias towards a blazing logged fire.

'Sit down,' said Wilhelm. 'Please, be my guest. A glass?' Tobias declined, settling himself instead into one of the two slouchy tweed chairs that faced each other by the fire. In the house that Tobias had known since he was a boy, he sat opposite the man who had represented his father, and noticed an altered look in Wilhelm's eye. The agent, who he felt had never held out much hope for his efforts, stared at him now with glassy, ruddy pride, shook his head, sprouted tears of joy and drank fulsomely straight from the dark cerise wine bottle, talking on about how he had always, always known the boy had what his father had in him, how he and Claude had talked about the splinters of potential that had gurgled from Tobias's cot, how even as a small baby, they had seen it as clear as day. Tobias had it, he said, had always had it, since the day he was born.

Then the agent sat back, began to regale the ceiling, indulging himself with the past; stories about the part he had played in what might just become the highest selling father and son duo of the year. Wilhelm lauded over his own accomplishments; rambling on about how his smooth, delicate negotiations, his swift, deliberate moves, his impeccable sense of timing, his business acumen, had been the doing of it. The sounds Wilhelm made became low, almost inaudible, as if there was cotton wool now plugged into Tobias's ears.

Staring ahead into the fire, Tobias foresaw his own inferno, his thoughts snapping like the burning logs. They went round and round, as if his brain was wedged on a nightmarish carousel that could no longer rotate, but only clack repeatedly against a rusty hasp. His distress had started when Wilhelm had mentioned a name he knew only too well, that of the megalith of critics, the one and only Jeffrey Stein. How was he going to deflect the sword fight of questions that The Times of New York City critic Jeffrey Stein was no doubt sharpening his pen for? How was he going to talk convincingly about a book that he didn't even write? With flights already booked, it was a bind from which he saw no escape.

The night-time Manhattan skyline was articulate; a yellow Rubik's Cube of windows behind which the silhouette of a million lives played out in framed rows; serried back-lit boxes that stacked into bigger rectangles, then stood up vertically and shot off in angles toward the sky. Stein crumpled his forehead, glanced at the circulating snapping photographer, blinked, folded his arms and jerked back with interest when Tobias could not tell his own words from those of Flaubert, Emily Dickenson, or Robert Frost, whose floral writing he had paralleled against the book. Throughout the interview Tobias sat molded to his seat, imagined the intersecting wires beneath him buckling, the giving way of fiberglass deception, the exposing cracks that might at any moment bottom out the heap of lies on which he sat, sending him toppling to the floor. He side-eyed Wilhelm, a pleading glance, immediately met with action. The agent charged forward, breaking the conversation by lamping a sturdy paternal hand on his client's shoulder, followed by an inflexible declaration. 'That's enough for today.'

Chapter 12

1990, February Berlin

'Since the arrival of Tobias Pilzerhoff 's The Scent of Heaven, the world has become one big botanic episode. Everyone is "doing foliage" this year, and everyone seems to know a whole lot more about it than they did last year – everyone except Tobias Pilzerhoff, that is.

Having forked out to have Pilzerhoff, and his profligate agent (as well as the agent's wife) flown first class from Berlin to New York to answer my questions, I expected more. Frankly, I feel I've been gamed. It's my personal expense account that is trousering the bill for the most pricey rooms in town for Master Pilzerhoff (et al.) But that's not the core issue here. It's more a problem of repetition. When asked to describe the book's premise, backstory, inspiration and strategy, Tobias Pilzerhoff robotically duck dives the questions. "I am thrilled that literary techniques and botany are now part of the dialogue amongst the wider community," he tells me. It's a spiel I have heard no less than three times, since it served as his riposte to three different questions already. Pilzerhoff seems to be sticking to some ready-made answers designed to deflect all discourse. He is a master prevaricator, a man running on a rehearsed narrative that supersedes all engagement.

It begs the question what is he hiding. Prevarication is an art form usually reserved for political leaders, those guarding state secrets, or with something worse to conceal. Unless he is masking something, it remains a mystery, therefore, why this author repeats the same thing in different ways regardless of the question posed.

I've seen some atrociously bad speakers in my time, some of them nonetheless excellent writers, but the pile of whizzing mold that Tobias Pilzerhoff patters off to describe the rationale of a backstory – well, it has left me with only one question: Does he himself actually believe any of what he is saying? Given that he does not engage in anything that could be called a discussion about the book, it is hard to believe he even wrote it. The longer I converse with Pilzerhoff, the stronger the whiff gets. And not of heaven, but rather more like the stink of something farm animals produce in abundance.'

Masticating his way in head-shaking disapproval down to the last sentence of The Times of New York City article, Wilhelm finally turned to him. 'Better to stay away from the newspapers,' Tobias nodded, then breathed an internalized sigh of relief.

'Why promote a book that has already topped Der Spiegel bestseller list anyway?' Wilhelm added, folding the paper before slapping it down on the sofa beside Tobias and himself with cheerful finality.

'Do they expect a man to remember every single word he writes?' he said to nobody in particular. Tobias nodded, willing this line of thinking on. 'Why not take a break, Tobias? Go to the mountains? Better to be out of the public eye right now. Too much noise and hype. It can't be good for your creativity. I should imagine it must be draining.' Again, Tobias nodded.

'They don't understand a man of your talent. They make too much of every small stutter, every tiny faux pas because they can't understand that people of finely tuned intellectual instrumentation are not like themselves, do not work by battery like TV screens that can be switched on and off with the press of a little button.'

'You're right, they don't understand,' said Tobias, shaking his head.

'Have you thought about what you will do? You are a rich man now, Tobias. You could write some more books, or focus on finding someone, you know, a woman, or... whatever?'

Tobias stared out the window, considering for the first time the possibilities now open to him.

'There's a house.'

'Oh yes?' said Wilhelm.

'Actually, it's more of a Schloss, a fine place, built in the Middle Ages for a noble man, something of a fortress.'

'To live in a castle. Why not? Where exactly is this place? 'Just outside Düsseldorf.'

'You will go to look at it, will you? 'I believe I will.'

'You could take the train.'

'Yes. That is just what I will do. Tomorrow. I'll go early.'

Chapter 13

June, 1990, Schloss Ludwig, Düsseldorf

It was called Schloss Ludwig because it was built for a prince on the anniversary of the eponymous Kings coronation. He and his progeny lived there for the best part of a century. In about 1944, the plot had been seized by Nazis. They used it to service the war effort; for meetings, storage of artillery and the like. Some senior military officers stayed there occasionally, but more often than not, it went unused.

In recent years, the German state had claimed Schloss Ludwig along with its impressive tinder forest surroundings, but they could not sell it, as they didn't have the original deeds – paperwork that lay in a dusty office somewhere in East Berlin, hidden behind the Berlin Wall until 1989. Repatriation was also an issue; there was talk of the original family coming back to claim it. So, there it sat, dank and empty, uninhabited since 1944. It was only after the Berlin Wall came down that the property came up for public auction, and only after, mind, an adjustments officer from Berlin had taken a trip out to Namibia to search for the Prince's progeny, to check if any of them had survived, in which case the holdings would be duly theirs. It turned out that the last of them had passed on, so the castle was free of any liens or potential disputes. Even so, most people didn't fancy living in that musty old place full of memories. And therefore Tobias got it for a steal. Immediately after the sale, he moved in and sequestered himself into one of the fairy-tale turrets which, by early Summer, he had acquired the deeds of. The same deal that had closed the heavy iron gates of that fortress behind him, opened for Tobias a chance to let his hair down – and with it, his guard - and withdraw from the invasive eyes of society.

His idea was to enforce a boundary, put up bastions and a heavy gate to keep out intrusions such as, 'How did you keep the writing of your novel a secret from your entire family and literary agent?' and, 'When are you going to write a sequel to The Scent of Heaven ?' as well as the unsettling,'Where did you get the idea from?', the infuriating, 'None of your contemporaries at university remember you having much of an interest in botany or gardening?', the utterly repugnant, 'When did you do all that research about flowers and plants?' and, lastly, the severely irritating, 'The writing style of your other book is nothing like The Scent of Heaven. How come?'

Wilhelm welcomed the news of Tobias's retreat to a castle high in the hills somewhere near Düsseldorf. He took the opportunity to have an official photograph of Tobias commissioned, just one mind. Then he followed it up with a press release; a carefully drafted document evincing Tobias's inspiration for the novel, the emotions and themes that the artist was attempting to channel therein, his personal philosophy and life-long interest in nature, hiking and the great outdoors, pursuits that he had enjoyed with his father. The agent hoped those breadcrumbs of truth embedded in the document would put to rest the incongruity of his client's previous, clumsy responses when interviewed about his prose.

Wilhelm painted Tobias as a rare genius, a shy man of few words, who did not speak in public due to his very sensitive disposition, a reclusive creative sort, living now in an undisclosed location to work intensely on a new book. These actions, the agent mused, no doubt would reduce interest in the novel and its author. Such would be a loss, one he would have to soak up to ensure no more disastrous press episodes that reflected badly on himself by linking him to an ineloquent buffoon who didn't seem to have a conceptual framework, a theoretical case study or any other preliminary research to explain the highly evocative and much revered book he had written.

Now Tobias lounged about the banqueting hall of Schloss Ludvig most days. Like some plutocrat, or lord of days gone by, he sat sometimes alone in the capacious library typing, or walked the park of rare trees, documenting species that inhabited his land. Or he stood, hands behind his back, gazing at the glassy lake and picturesque forests. On fine afternoons he sometimes drove to the city of Düsseldorf, the capital of North Rhine-Westphalia, or took the motorway to Brussels to look about the shops and amuse himself with some pleasurable activity or other.

For almost a month he did not entertain one visitor, did not hear the gravelly interruption of a car on his drive, did not find himself inundated with junk mail of invitations and requests, and was for those reasons quite sure that members of the public or press did not know his whereabouts or, better still, had moved on, forgotten about him altogether. That was until the doorbell's gong interrupted his wishful thinking, its over-zealous chiming harmony bringing tidings of a visitor's announcement, a gong that introduced itself in every room simultaneously, with just one uninvited single- finger press of the round button outside his door.

'Good day, Mr. Pilzerhoff. I am your postman. Didn't think you would answer the door.'

'Ah yes. Can I help you?' Tobias put his head out from behind the heavy panelled wood and looked around.

'I have this letter for you.'

'Did you not see the letter box at the gate?' said Tobias. 'It must be signed for, though. Sorry to intrude. You see,here?'

'Indeed. So, I will make an exception today, but normally post goes in the box provided.' said Tobias, taking the paper. Tobias scribbled his signature with incipient misery, brought on by the realization that his asylum had been breached. Then he took the letter inside and opened it. The card said that the Deutscher Buchpreis, awarded annually in October by the Börsenverein des Deutschen Buchhandels, had been won by The Scent of Heaven. Taking a seat at his typewriter, he read the letter a second time, then began

writing one of his own to say that he would not be accepting the prize, and not to contact him again about the matter. A few weeks later, the same ebullient post-man pushed his bicycle up the winding lane and rang the truculent bell, and again he handed to Tobias an envelope with a signatory requirement. Tobias took it in, opened it, and responded similarly to whoever it was that organized the Goethe prize. To this reply he jotted up a similar riposte as before but added that he did not need the sizeable prize pot mentioned, and was quite happy for them to give the money to someone who did, so long as they did not expect him to take hand, act or part in the process. Again, he requested with servile

politeness not to be disturbed about the matter further.

By the end of the month, the name Tobias Pilzerhoff was back in the papers, not just in Germany but across the globe.

The press had laid their hands on a copy of 'The Tobias Pilzerhoff Refusal Letter,' and had taken quotes from it. Among the thinking classes, the act of rejecting the prizes had been interpreted as a humble, charitable declaration, an act that demonstrated socialist leanings; the work of a man preoccupied with fair distribution of wealth. Now an outcry of support for an 'International Literary Treasure' rang out, Tobias at its center. His humility, generosity and grace, they claimed, deserved not only the prizes that had already been offered – those which he had so graciously declined – but even greater prizes, the biggest of all, in fact. There was even talk, in one article, of a Nobel Prize for Literature.

Chapter 14

August, 1990, Schloss Ludwig, near Düsseldorf

Castle Ludwig boasted no less than ten bedrooms, all of which were decorated as if three swashbuckling musketeers might pounce out from behind a heavy wardrobe at any time. In each of the bedrooms there hung swag-tail pelmet curtains, a black wrath iron electrified candelabra. In the center of the rooms was an enormous hand carved linen dressed four-poster bed of solid oak. The fittings made Tobias think of a story; about a young woman whose noble heritage was revealed through her ability to detect a minuscule bump underneath a stack of duvets. Tonight, he lay awake as that same fairytale princess did, tossing and turning in his luxurious castle bed, unable to settle the irascible pea of moral discontent lodged within the vaults of his mind.

The book whose story had brought this luxury his way, was the cause of his ire. He had done nothing wrong, really, but he had not done anything right either. He had merely transcribed a document, and now he was living the life of a prince on the proceeds of words that did not belong to him but to someone else, some forgotten child. He would never know that person, and yet that girl had influenced the course of his life. What sensibility had driven her to write those enchanting chronicles sleeping as she did on a harsh makeshift bed, a cold plank of injustice, with nothing but sackcloth rags to cover her frail body? Somehow, the girl had found something beyond the brutality of her circumstances. She had spun a bountiful silk duvet of visionary expression, words so well crafted and pure that the entire world had fallen in love with love again.

In a bid to relieve his discomfort, Tobias tossed and tumbled once more. With this new position came another viewpoint. Was he not the skilled translator who had given the writer of a forgotten manuscript the chance to live again, who had liberated her from the grave? Without his input, that document would surely have burned on a pyre, or ended up in a filthy bin. He had taken a risk, had wandered outside the academic standard, had linked his name to writings that pressed on irrational, unquantifiable points; had associated himself with snub-worthy topics, admissions of admiration, the longing for physical human closeness; had exposed himself as frail, vulnerable even.

Just because it had gone right did not take away from the gamble, the risk to his reputation. Innocent rudimentary plot lines about perfume, and flowers; they could have cost him his academic reputation. Afterall, he hadn't only translated that story, he had patched up the narrative too. It had taken time to correct its failings, the anachronistic problems, technical concerns, discordant imaginary that historians and botanists would surely not have missed. It had been incorrectly punctuated, fraught with spelling errors, had contained issues with commas and hyphens that would not have been overlooked. Yes, she had written something noteworthy that brought forward a new idea, but he had structured it with cold hard research, with historical precision, had fitted it out with a suitable choice of language.

Was he not part of the story then? Even if he wasn't the sole hero that people thought him now; at the very least had his gallant actions – his education, his erudite ability to identify poignant exposition – not led to the manuscript's reinvigoration so that the entire world could, almost half a century later, savor its rough beauty?

He had mined a crude gem, had brought it out of the mud, wedged apart a clam, unearthed the pearl, but he might have sullied himself. It was a punt, like all of life, a stroke of luck that came from an investment on his part. Sure, it had been fruitful, and now he was living with the glory that came of his efforts. He had been crowned as the fellow who had re-acculturated romance and passion, made such notions fashionable again. The book had prompted others to consume those lost topics, had awakened a repressed and ageless pang, a desire for bewildering longing, for unlikely, queer, illogical, chaotic, eccentric, unbridled love.

He had stolen nothing. That manuscript had come to him. He sat on the side of his bed now, the document in his hand, flipping through its shabby, brittle pages. But the fact of not recognizing her ghost, was that not in itself a crime? He did not know that girl, could not even think how he might find out about her. There were, after all, no leads, no inscriptions to assist him. Still, the pea of moral discontent prodded at him, bruising the fragile self image of the man of upstanding ethics that he thought himself to be.

What was he to do? How might he fix it? A proviso was needed. If that girl could speak from the grave, what would she say? What would she ask of him? He sat in silence, staring at the ceiling. If she could speak from the grave… the grave, where was her grave? That was it, she had no grave. Then, it came to him. Of course. Why did he not think of it before? No memorial for her life existed, so he would make one. Although, he would never know the fate of the manuscript's author after she had entered that awful place, he could at least make her a headstone, a place for him to go to kneel, and talk to her, and tell her how her words had changed the world. That he could do. He would give that girl the ceremonial send-off she deserved. He would choose a place right here on the grounds of Schloss Ludwig, dig out a void, line it with concrete, and make a proper tomb; have a sculpture commissioned to go with it, a symbolic dedication. The manuscript would be placed there as a memorial, sealed up forever in the earth. That was what he was going to do. From that four-poster bed, he made a promise to build it with his own hands so that he might personally honor her, and give the credit back. It would be her place, somewhere to be, a home, well for her spirit at least. And a place where he could talk to that author, appease her, and settle the score.

It was easier, once he could visualize that memorial in his mind's eye, to be at peace, to come to terms with the book, and to admit to himself that he was only the translator; not the great humanitarian, not the great writer, not the one deserving of a prize or a castle, of a four-poster bed or any of the things that the world had given him. He could digest it all now with equanimity, because of the memorial, because he could do something, give something back. With thoughts of that mausoleum in his mind, Tobias Pilzerhoff melted into a decompressing sigh, and, for the first time in weeks, dozed peacefully. That night he slept like a boy in his cot, one who had just had a fairy tale read to him. He pulled the feathery duvet around himself, and within minutes was snoring aloud.

Chapter 15

June, 1989, Berlin

During the First World War, a soldier called Adolf was in the trenches. He reported that he heard a voice say 'move.' If he hadn't moved when he heard that voice, or so the story goes he would have been blown up like the rest of his colleagues. Chance was a fine thing. Helmut Englehaus came to that view after roaming from place to place wondering what to do with his life in his post-army years, the interregnum before establishing Müller's Chocolate Palais, and settling in Brussels. Helmut Englehaus loved stories, especially stories about chance events.

Loulita Hirsch also loved stories. She collected them in her head, filed them away to later chimera them into the fabric of her novels. Very soon, her own story would merge with Helmut's by chance, but today she was in Berlin's Jewish Museum, had seen enough of that building's brutal voids, and taken in one too many of the dead-end finalities and sorrowful endings that it housed.

If she had been born just a few decades earlier, Loulita Hirsch might have had to wear the yellow star; and her own story might have ended behind Perspex in a museum, or been forgotten altogether.

Her distant ancestors came to Germany after the Alhambra Decree of 1492. A second wave of relatives sought refuge in Frankfurt in the 1880s when the Pogroms ripped through the Russian Empire. Up to 1939, the Hirsch's had been book people. Her grandparents had gotten out before Frankfurt fell, a sagacious move, and one that paved the way for Loulita's birth and survival. Only one of them had stepped up after the war when Grandfather Abraham Hirsch returned from exile to claim the boarded-up shop in Frankfurt. That was Samuel, her father.

Although she never knew Grandfather Hirsch, Loulita was born in Frankfurt. Abraham Hirsch had re-established Hirsch's bookshop from the ashes of the former pre-war book shop business, and re-installed the family above the shop when the fighting ended. Then the accident happened, and her Aunt Kitty came. For Loulita and her sister to lose both parents so tragically seemed even more cruel considering what their Grandparents had lived through. 'God only takes the best.' Aunt Kitty had said, but it only made her more angry at Him.

It was expected that Loulita Hirsch would by now be cosseting a husband, and running a gaggle of children like her sister. But she wasn't because part of her commuted to other worlds, leaving only fifty percent of her to inhabit this one. She was blessed or cursed with the makeup of a natural-born story smith, traits that add complexity to one's corporeal everyday existence.

The hollow face when painted with a dusting of rogue made her look closer to thirty, or so people said, but she had been around for ten years more. It could have been the bright colors that she chose that threw them off, or her bird-like skeletal frame. Green was her favorite. Today she wore her forest green gabardine, the chestnut brown hair swept off her face, her dark oval eyes soulful and haunted under blackout sunglasses.

Wandering north up Berlin's Lindenstraße, the dizziness came over her, and she stopped to grip a wall. A slug of water from the bottle in her handbag would get her to Oranienstraße, where she might sit down, and take a black coffee, but no food. When the dizziness passed, Loulita walked on, arriving at a stark angular city street which gave way to a kaleidoscope of painted shops, the relief of one-man-show coffee peddlers, and eventually a road given over to pedestrians and cyclists. Chancing towards a small, graffiti painted bistro, she entered to ask about a vacancy, but could not speak above the thumping music, the plates and cups reverberating. Incandescent bulbs glared into her eyes, and she turned back toward the door, and left.

Further along the stretch, she drifted in the direction of a scent. Led by her nose to a doorway where a Damascus rose oil burner steamed over a tea-light, Loulita's senses capitulated, and she allowed them to pull her down some steps into the quiet shelter of a subterranean bookshop, a place with creaky floor-boards, Shanti music, rag-rugs, freestanding shelves, alms of philosophy, and a prismatic menagerie of glass bottles.

Lost amongst those quixotic things – books of aged leather and objets d'art – her lungs fed on the scented air, and she picked out a hardback. Loulita soon became so engrossed that she did not notice the vendor's voice, and was startled to find him standing close to her. 'May I help you with something?' said the little man.

'Oh, no, no, I was just looking, thank you,' said Loulita. 'That book, the one you have selected, it is for someone

looking for a place, the right place.'

'Is it?' asked Loulita. The man nodded. 'Is that you?'

'Well, I don't know. You could say that, I suppose, about anyone,' she said, closing the book before slotting it back

into the shelf.

'What place are you looking for, if I may ask?' said the man. 'Ah, no,' said Loulita. 'I'm not... really. I just came in to

browse.'

'You are looking for a place, I think,' said the man.

'Well, no. But I am looking for a job, but I don't think I will find that in a book,' laughed Loulita.

'You are looking for a job in Berlin?' 'Yes, I am.'

'How do you know that you are in the right city, though?' 'I'm sorry. I don't know what you mean?

'May I ask what it is that you do?'

'Well, I do many things, and there are many jobs in Berlin, are there not?' The man nodded.

'So I suppose I am in the right city then,' Loulita smiled at him and moved towards the door.

'Yes, perhaps,' said the man, 'but you may not be on the line for the right job in the right city, if you follow my meaning.' 'The correct line? Like a train line?' said Loulita, turning around.

'No,' said the man. 'That book, the one you were reading,

The Zodiac of Travel?'

'Oh,' she said. 'No, I...' she laughed. 'Well, I was just looking.' The man smiled at her.

'Then why did you come in here? Why did you pick up that particular book, and read it like the rest of the world had disappeared around you?'

'Oh, well… I do things like that sometimes… a lot, actually."

'Do you?' said the man.

'Yes, it was just a… a chance thing. I have notions of writing books,' laughed Loulita.

'A chance thing?' said the man, raising his brows.

'Yes, chance,' said Loulita, a hotness spreading across her face now.

'Well, thanks. I best be off then.'

The man walked back toward the counter. Going behind it, he took to his stool, and resumed his own reading. Loulita placed a foot on the first rung of the stairs, then looked back at him, and he nodded to her as she began the climb toward the street. For the next three days, Loulita enquired about employment at no less than a dozen bistros, and no less than a dozen times her courteous enquiry met equally courteous head-shaking. She did not want to drive her taxi in Berlin. That was not supposed to be her job, not now that she was… what was she? A woman with nearly four decades to her name, and nothing to show for it? That's what she was now. Driving a taxi was a novel thing to do for a rebellious young woman, a hip sideline for a person who was really a writer. When she told her passengers about her real job, their next question was always the same. 'Written anything I would know? 'The person used to ask, 'I'll look out for your book. What's your name?' But lately, because perhaps she had lost her enthusiasm for the dream, they just looked out the window when she talked of her other career. And Loulita would find herself bumbling on as if to convince them – or herself – by saying that she was still looking for the right agent. After that, their eyes would glaze over; become languid with disinterest, an expression that let her know that they had decided she was that sort of writer, the sort that had never been published, and could not make any money with their flimsy stories. They would know then that no one cared to read her scribbles, that her stories were awful, and so she stopped saying that she was a writer, and had, in fact, all but stopped believing that she was a writer too.

Driving the taxi was supposed to be a stop-gap, something that would enable her to save some money, get out and about, meet people, hear their stories, and write. Instead, it had become part of her identity. In Frankfurt, people on her street thought of her as 'that woman who drives a taxi,' not 'that writer who has a dozen books waiting to be published.' Driving the cab had become indelibly tangled up with who she was, and this was the reason that she needed to start again in a new city. She was tired of struggling, and since she had written all the books she ever wanted to write, and gotten nowhere with them, it was time to find an easier life. A stable life in a different city where nobody knew or cared about her failings. A place that would allow her to sit in a chair in the evenings, and get old if that was what life had in store.

Sharing a room, or living at home were no longer options. That had been done, and out-done for long enough. Now, the time had arrived to find herself somewhere to belong, to establish herself in some arboreal lodging that she might climb up into, and ease her bones at the end of the day, a place where she might install her books, as well as the other belongings that she had been carting around from flat to flat in a battered suitcase.

At the bottom of that flimsy trunk was the box of old letters left to her by her aunty. It seemed like an eternity since her aunt's death, and England. But it had only happened in January. Berlin would get five more days of her efforts. By day four, she was back on Oranienstraße, and had reunited with the trailing scent of Damascus rose. This time the bookshop owner was standing in his doorway.

'Hello again,' he said, nodding at her as she passed the shop. 'Have you found that "right job" yet?'

'No, nothing at all,' said Loulita. 'Your oil smell so good.' 'Syrian Roses,' said the man. 'Perhaps you are looking in the wrong place, for the job, I mean.'

'I don't follow,' said Loulita.

'There is a right place and a wrong place for all things, you know?'

'I'd like to believe that, but I've given in to dreamy fantasies for long enough, and, well, they haven't gotten me very far.'

'Nothing happens by chance.'

'You think so?'

'Come. I will show you,' said the man. Loulita stood on the doorstep scratching her head. She looked out at the street, then back into the shop, but the man was already halfway down the stairs.

'Well?' he said up at her.

Loulita did not move. Then the fluid-filled sac of blistering soreness on her right heel began to pulsate, reminding her of the long walk back to her hostel, and so, with a deep breath, she descended the steps following the gentle padding motion of the man's feet. Taking a seat opposite him, her heel celebrated the relief.

'So What are you going to do to me? Tell my fortune?' she asked, making big eyes to demonstrate her cynicism.

'Not exactly.'

'What am I doing back here then?'

'You were compelled to return here. Nothing to do with me. I am only going to help you to understand what it was that you came back here for,' the man explained.

'I wish my life was as enchanted as the way you make it sound. But I am just another person looking for a job to pay the bills, and this is where the cafés and shops are, so I...'

'Is that so?' said the man.

'I'm sad to admit it, and only wish I had something more captivating to tell you, but I only came in because my feet...' She looked at his hand, the expectantly held pencil, and stopped talking. Then the nebulous, illogical, watery quality of her imagination took hold, and she wanted to believe in something nacreous like the crystals that hung about the shop, something opaque and mysterious like the sporadic melodies that tickled the wind chimes by the door. Then came over her a fulminating urge to be swished away by some visceral notion of destiny, a longing to believe in the simplicity of a predetermined life path. Giving herself over to her nature, she blurted out the answers to the discordant set of particulars that the man requested of her with a nonchalant eagerness.

He needed to know her birthday, including the exact time of birth, then he skirted some calculations around on a piece of paper, and after some time looked up and advised Loulita

Hirsch that, based on the details she had provided, Brussels would offer more benevolent opportunities than Berlin

'Brussels?'

'In Brussels there is optimal achievement potential for a job, and to grow,' said the man. 'A stay there would be highly recommended if self-confidence has been depleted,' he continued. University came floating back to her. 'Especially if some foe's recent attack has damaged the spirit.'

Some foe indeed. Try a dozen aspirant critics, she thought, a coterie given to outdoing each other in the realm of spiteful commentary, an ersatz talent, a deflection from their own writing.

'Tricksters seem to be at every corner, do they not?'
'Admittedly. But I suppose that could be applied to

anyone's life, not just mine,' said Loulita, waking up to the possibility that she was probably going to be hit with a bill next.

'Look, do I need to pay you something at the end?' The man glanced at her over his glasses, but made no comment for some time. Then he spoke.

'I invited you, did I not?' She had never thought of it being a con until now.

'Yeah but, I would need to go to the bank if...' The man raised his grey eyebrows, and she noticed the clarity in his eyes.

'Only four hundred Mark. Is that alright?' 'I don't have ..look, I thought this was...'

'Not everyone in the world is a hoodwinker, you know,' said the man.

'What?'

'You can trust some people. Not all of them, but some.' 'So you are not going to charge me, then?'

'There is no fee.'

'Oh, Ok, I just thought you might...'

'Does it feel like the world is against you sometimes, Loulita?' said the man, pointing down at the drawing he had made, the circle and lines that apparently told him something about her life. She shrugged and sighed.

'I suppose it does,' she said.

'It hasn't been an easy road for you so far, but it will get better.' At his words of kindness, Loulita felt her shoulders drop. A gulp came into her throat, and she wanted to cry, but held back the latent well.

'That's all behind you.'

'Is it? Is it really?' she looked up at the man.

'Really, it is. You will meet a friend in Brussels. He will give you something, and you will give him something in return,'

'He?' The bookseller nodded.

'Oh no. I'm not looking for anything like that.' 'Nobody can do it all by themselves, Loulita.'

'I would rather try with the luck I've had...' 'There are better times ahead.'

The man went on to talk about his own life. When she looked up towards the window, Loulita could see that it was already dark outside; time to go. Back at the hostel, she sat on the edge of the hard dormitory bed. Two of her room colleagues - French, she guessed by their effortless style and nymph-like beauty - had just returned from the showers. They stood now before her, naked, conversing, Loulita baring the awkwardness by looking at her shoes as one of the girls applied black eyeliner, and the other back-combed her hair in the mirror, squirting sporadic sticky fugues of hairspray into the air. The gauze of acetate on contact with Loulita's lungs caused an explosion of coughs, and the two dormitory companions became mute, fixing their stares her way. The road beckoned. Her foot twitched. The girls went back to their toilette. Four minutes later, Loulita Hirsch had picked up her wash bag, put her toothbrush inside it, zipped up her luggage, placed everything she owned into the battered suitcase that was now being dragged downstairs. After paying her bill, she left the hostel, and was soon behind the wheel of the parked yellow cab. Hands at the helm, and ready to go, she sighed aloud, then peered up at the sky. A slither of silver moon arched against a navy background. Five thousand years, the man had said; that is how long people had been looking into the night sky and gleaning significance from what they saw.

Twenty-five minutes later, the Autobahn was ahead of her. A few hours on, Berlin was a spatter of orange flecks behind her, black trees encasing the road ahead like some sort of gothic black hole of past and future. She peered out the window, up towards a tiny light on the mountain ahead. High in the distant forested hills, that lit pinhead glowed yellow. Then it went black, causing an involuntary jump because a person was up there, and because they too were awake at this time, that unknown soul living high in the hills. Amongst that cluster of inky spruces, the ghostly transfer of Schloss Ludwig came into full view a few minutes on, its pointed fairytale turrets against a sapphire and diamond night. Then another yellow dot blinked on in a different quarter of the building. That dot of gold ahead made her heart leap a second time, and again she didn't know why. Some hours later she reached Brussels Centraal, and parked up near the station, where she was met with a blast of sharp morning air. The buckled strap of her carry-all bag digging into her shoulder, the old suitcase with the box of letters and photographs inside rattling over cobblestone, she walked from the car park towards the citadels nucleus. Jumping the bag onto her back, she paused every few hundred meters, then meandered to the main quarter of Brussels, trudging onto a narrow lane. The big hand of the city clock moved towards six. She had driven through the night. Now it was the next day. Around The Grand Place, baristas began to rattle keys in doors, while dough-bellied restaurant chefs wiped sleep from their eyes, and started up ovens.

She found a hotel, was buzzed into its foyer, then crossed a cold mosaic floor, climbed a wooden set of stairs, shivering herself rid of the chilled morning air. At the top, a woman with short dark hair unlatched an apartment from which orange light streamed the corridor, and the warm smell of a wood fire relaxed the air. Loulita signed a form, showed her passport, and followed the woman to her lodgings.

'You will be staying with us for how long?' enquired the hotelier.

'I don't know,' said Loulita, turning her face to the colossal oil paintings on high-ceilinged gallery walls, glancing at portraits in gold frames against a wallpaper of crimson velvet damask as they walked through room after room.

'This place is old?' she said. The woman nodded.

'Your room is in here,' she said, pushing a key into a heavy door. Loulita entered, walked to the window, and stood in front of a balcony.

May I?' she asked, before releasing the delicate brass latch that led out onto a rectangular veranda, enclosed in a filigree metal railing. It extended over the grand square below. The woman left, did not witness therefore the breath of awe that filled Loulita's nostrils, or the straightening up of her back at the sight that opened up before her of the city below. She turned around to address the hotelier, 'How much is this apartment?' she said to an empty room.

There was a card of prices and services on the bed. This huge space was less than what she was paying in Berlin to share a dormitory. She had a sense that she was paying over the odds, but never thought to check with the other residents. Loulita stepped out onto the granite paved shelf balcony to survey the alternating guildhalls and private houses of Brussels' Grand Square. Gripping the metal railing not to hold on but to suppress a swoon brought about by the proximity of so much splendid craftsmanship all at once, she panned the edifices.

On all sides now were ornate façades, sculptured pilasters, delicate plaster work, articulated window boxes and doorways; rows of marble balustrades, lavish carved shells, chimeras, gargoyles and floral engravings that came to life around her; flowers unfurling, cupids bowing their heads. She sat on the bed. A benevolent windfall of chance, an impulsive illogical split-second decision had landed her on her feet.

Facing the open balcony doors in front, a warm wind feathered her face, and a ray of sunshine settled the air. She pulled the olfactory city into her lungs, then climbed under the covers, and slept through the day.

Chapter 16

June, 1989, Schloss Ludwig, Düsseldorf

When Tobias was a small boy, Ingrid had read nightly to him fairytales gathered and written down by two brothers named Grimm; stories of goblins and trolls who lurked in places just off the path. It was these tales which set the man up philosophically.

To this day, Tobias still, although quite unaware that he was doing it, viewed the world through a subconscious paved out of the moralistic bye-laws of those writings. His adult eyes sought sign-posted pathways where the way ahead was lit. He valued scruples reminiscent of a bygone era. Of course, he no longer believed in fairies, witches, dwarves and elves, but remnants of those phantoms still inhabited the deepest recesses of his adult mind. The childish belief had matured into its equivalent grown-up value, a meditation on cause and effect, a stoicism manifested into habits, a preoccupation with planning and strategy. Much contemplation came in advance of action. By doing things right, he believed, the sinuous path of uncertainty might be chartered, navigated and ultimately managed. If a man was to build a tomb, it should be a tomb worth building, a well constructed edifice in precisely the right location so that it would endure the challenges of time eternal. Such were Tobias's thoughts as he put on his walking shoes, took a hiking pole and perambulated the grounds around Schloss Ludwig in search of just the right place, one befitting of a burial plot for the manuscript. As he went on his way, he took the opportunity to note any changes, such as a tree whose branches required pruning back or had begun to sag. For such observations, he kept a notebook in the pocket of his cargo pants so that he would remember the exact spot when he returned to that matter in the future.

As he trudged the fields, stopping here and there to inspect some vegetation or fencing, the flicker of an idea came into his mind. Once this business with the manuscript was done; once that contentious document was ceremoniously buried and forgotten about, Blossoms would be born. According to him, The Scent of Heaven could do with improvement. He had been studying it since the Stein incident and had found it fraught with errors and inaccuracies. For example, in Chapter Eighteen, there was a line that went, 'The delicate, soft kiss of the first day of a season.' For one thing, seasons did not 'kiss' anyone. It didn't make sense. Although Tobias was a fine editor, sometimes the subtlety of language was lost on him because of his need for flat, one-dimensional meanings, combined with a fervent, all consuming desire to be right. Contemplation on any meaning other than the most widely accepted one of the day was sophism, according to him. This leaning towards compliance saw him right most of the time with translations, only that in a very ancient language like Hebrew, there are often several different possible meanings for the same word depending on context. For example, the Hebrew word 'Moed' does not only mean 'seasons' but also conveys 'eternity.' There were in fact two ways to understand the sentence, 'The delicate, soft kiss of the first day of a season.'

True, even Tobias with his analogous mindset, would concede that the precise definition of the original word for 'season' had shifted marginally to refer to a time period when seeds are sown - that some poetic gratuity should be applied. Only it suited him now to find fault with the work, and so he told himself, therefore, that any academic who had studied languages to a reputable level – as he had – could not go against the debate that The Scent of Heaven lacked methodical exactness.

Even though it was himself who had originally translated the manuscript Tobias, prone as he was to ignoratio elenchi, a penchant towards the missing of the point, concluded that any person of noble standing would have to agree - when the 'tangible facts' were laid out before them, referenced in a bibliography, an exercise which Tobias Pilzerhoff was more than willing to undertake to prove his point - that there was an urgent need for a redaction, and for another more scientific version of the book.

108

Moreover, if such news about him had been printed, written and published in a respected newspaper, laid out in black and white beside a photograph of his face, and an article typed up stating that he was working on a follow-up to The Scent of Heaven, then not only was it reasonable to respond to an article like that by doing that very thing, but also it was his duty to do so.

If people were so given with flowers and scents, then surely what was called for was a more accurate story; a mature, non-sentimental take to elucidate them around those topics, a didactic novel, one that would turn a new chapter in the history of that cherished book, with the added bonus of being factually correct when it came down to details. Blossoms, his new book, would offer all that. It would serve accuracy, have an ebullient narrative built on sequential movement, and would therefore appeal to the sensibilities of the serious man, the serious writer, like the man his father had been.

He was not rejecting the first book by any means. No. He was not arguing that it was not somewhat contributory. It had its place. Therefore, he would not start some revisionist campaign that would lead to it being pulled off the shelves or act with any other such unrestrained a flamme. No, no. Not at all. Some interesting concepts lay inside those pages, for sure. Besides, hard work had been invested into writing the book, and hard work was something Tobias Pilzerhoff respected even if the final product did not meet his own personal tastes or come up to his intellectual standards.

There was a case for enduring those words under his own name if that was what it took for them to remain available to the public. Since the proletariat, he reasoned, derived so much enjoyment from that book, who was he to thwart their follies? He was only the one in charge of those words, the man who authorized their print runs, accepted royalties, put his name to them. On the other hand, he was also the one who took creative responsibility for all their puerile inadequacies, and so it was high time that he made a start on a follow-up.

But before Blossoms would come into the world, the original manuscript had to be done away with, put to rest, given the funerary send-off that it deserved. And for that, he needed to find the right patch of ground. Such was the correct way to proceed, he admonished as he pushed his walking rod into the turf, tilted his chin skywards, made a forward swing with his right boot, and committed himself to the full force of his resolution.

Chapter 17

June, 1989, Brussels

Despite the evenings darkness, the outline of the city of Brussels beyond Loulita Hirsch's balcony window beckoned. After the long drive from Berlin, she had slept right through the day. Now that the circadian need for sleep had worn off, a walk was called for. What could be more thrilling than a night walk in a new city, she thought. The cool dusk smelled vaguely of woody smoke. Walking across Brussels' Grand Square, she stopped in front of a hanging flower basket laden with Evening Primrose, and took its scent. Having not yet discovered the town by day, she tried to imagine how it would look in the morning light. There were flowers everywhere. March had brought a flurrying spree of pinks along with purples, yellows and blues. Their colors hidden under darkness, the blooms sheltered in window boxes and on trellises, cheerful pastel color palettes kept secret for dawn to unveil. Night could not rob them of their most alluring charms. Their scent had survived. It suffused the air, swirling into an unseen petrichor. The bouquet was made up of a symphony of mixed botanicals. Hyacinths practiced a spring melody with bluebells, against jasmine that twisted around arches in hidden gardens where crocuses joined the troubadours of abundance, adding their own notes liberally.

Even though the day was well and truly over, people were still moving about inside the buildings around The Grand Square. Loulita could see the silhouetted outlines of men behind amber lit windows in the mansions around its perimeter; painters and gardeners, touching up stained glass. They were getting ready; standing on ladders, on scaffolding; pushing dusting cloths at corners to feather and sweep, working throughout the night. She took a seat at a late night café whose iron chairs and tables had not yet been fully withdrawn, and consulted the waiter.

'What is going on?' she said, nodding towards the workers.
'I don't understand, Miss,' said the maître d'.

'Why so much effort? The workers? It is late.'

'Ah yes. Summer is coming,' 'And...'

'You have never been in Brussels in the summertime, no?' She shook her head.

'Just you wait, then. It is the most rapturous place on earth.'

He had put it well, that maître d. Without a doubt, the city boasts a certain vitality at that time of year. It comes alive in part from all the new people, the visitors, from the flowers, from the shellfish and French fries, from the frothy beer, but above all it comes from the sweet exotic air produced by the cocoa that goes into the making of all that Belgian chocolate, the aroma of which wafts through the streets just under the discernible senses of its residents, but exuberantly noticeable to those who set foot there for the first time. Some don't smell it, or at least are not aware they do, but it still reaches them in some profound way, and alters their mood. A person of resolutely stern disposition becomes less so, the one who is content to start with, a fraction more. The syrupy air causes visitors to be less serious, to take on egalitarian, pliant leanings, to laugh at themselves, to make risible their own shortcomings, and to care less about how the world perceives them. It is this momentarily self-effacing liberation that causes visitors to invest in a funny tie, or a humorous keyring of a minuscule boy relieving his tiny metal bladder. Those things seem like fitting gifts, under the paroxysm of Brusselian chocolatey intoxication, for a boss, or a lover, or a wife, or the neighbor who minds the houseplants, except then the air is different in their respective home town, and on return the idea is curtly abandoned, the gifts banished to a no-mans-land drawer, to end their career in a charity shop. Under morning's spell, Brussels heaved to life. Plenitude bulged out all around, punctuated with the ameliorating din of hammers and saws. The sound sent waves of hope across the square, and Loulita filled up on it, as she did on the warm, fragranced, floral incursion of demerara, waffles, mocha, vanilla essence and toasty nuts.

The summer was on its way, alright, and that meant that the tourists were on their way too. Soon they would come in droves, coach-loads of them; trainfuls would arrive from the surrounding towns; from Antwerp, Cologne, Paris, Frankfurt, Nantes, Hamburg, Amsterdam and further, much further afield. They would cavalcade the narrow streets, park themselves up at some path side seat, roll up their sleeves and drink heady beer until late afternoon. Then they would meander and explore, before eventually ending up at Les Galeries Royales Saint-Hubert drinking hot chocolate, nibbling on truffles, nut ganache, nougat, dark oriental Turkish rose, brandy fudge, toffee, or spicy liqueurs. With a taste for the stuff, they would go on later to purchase chocolate in the smaller places on the cobbled lanes around; places like Helmut Englehaus's, or as the sign above the little door said, Müllers Palais de Praliné.

Müllers Palais de Praliné had opened its doors in early 1946, adding yet another chocolatier to the two thousand artisan makers and bake houses that already sprinkled the side streets of Brussels. When the signwriter asked what name Helmut Englehaus wanted above the door of his new confectionery shop, Mr. Englehaus chose the moniker written on the dairy product in his hand, rather than the one on his birth certificate. It was better that way. He was, from

114

then on Mr. Müller, a quiet man who didn't talk about his past, his time in the army, or mention that he had learned to cook in a German field kitchen, one that had ruthlessly confiscated food from the mouths of civilians in Belgium during the war. It was easier that people thought of him now as Mr. Müller. It was preferable that they presumed Mr. Müller to be a chocolatier from Switzerland, and not an ex-army chef from a small town in the north; better because some Brusseleers had not yet forgotten the sting of rations that came with occupations, and the hoarding of local supplies.

It was precisely because of the Second World War that Helmut had gone about finding a soulful occupation that he might conduct in a kitchen, and set his sights on the sweet ameliorating work of chocolate production. He had never believed in war, and living through one had not gone far to change his view. It had only sharpened his focus, and drawn up within him a steely determination to leave his army days far behind, to become someone else.

After the war, Helmut had spent many months deliberating, dreaming about what it was he might do now that the fighting had ceased. He had taken to peripatetic living, roaming around Europe, making simple sugar and butter toffee on a small camping stove at first, which he had then sold at markets in this town or that to get by. Children's faces had lit up with ruddy joy when he smuggled them a free piece, unbeknownst to their parents. If only he could have made the starving children smile. Still, their cadaverous faces haunted him at night, their bony hands reaching out for food, their vacant eyes. If he could have only saved one of them. He had almost saved a little girl. Almost.

After travelling around, living out of a bag, the road had taken Helmut Englehaus to Brussels, where he had worked at any job to pull together enough money to get a kitchen of his own off the ground. After securing his premises in Brussels, he had started by making muffins, brownies and cupcakes with bright colored sweets on top. Having put everything into the renting of this small shop with basic cooking space at the rear, he had not yet been able to afford the ingredients required to make pure Belgian chocolate. Cakes and pastries topped with high-sugar icing and cheap flavoring had given him his start. Despite being over-sweetened and containing only a splash of pure cocoa butter, they had been enough to ring in the first few coppers, and get his business moving in the right direction.

During those first few months, he had saved every coin that clanged into his till, and had purchased within a year a roasting oven, a device for cracking and winnowing his own beans. Then came the acquisition of an electric grinder, and later a tempering system. Once he was able to produce his own chocolate, his profits began to increase. With the proceeds, he had special molding trays commissioned, ones that embossed a prestigious M onto the dorsal of each truffle. He also installed a fan in his kitchen, with its vent facing out onto the street. He did this not because he needed to extract all that much condensation, but to entice customers inside by sending hot, melted chocolate and roasting cocoa steam onto the path of their nostrils. Each part of the truffle process had a set of instruments, which were laid out on the counter in advance along with the required ingredients and trays. It was this meticulous nature that ensured consistency in his product and led to mentions in magazines and papers as far away as Montreal of Müllers Palais de Praliné. Quite by chance, Müllers Palais de Praliné was the first place that Loulita Hirsch visited in Brussels about a job. For Helmut, the arrival of the peaky-faced gamine could not have come at a better time. When she smiled at him in acceptance of his proposal to 'give it a try', the sides of her eyes creased, lending a peppering of childlike vulnerability to her mien, one that pinged at Helmut's protective nature, bringing out in him some avuncular tendency. In any case, Loulita's arrival sent Helmut Englehaus into a celebratory mood, which drove him to perch himself at a bar after he locked up the shop that day, where he ordered a Cognac. Over that first Cognac, Helmut remembered all it had taken to get his little chocolate shop this far, how desperately he needed now an assistant to help him with the demand that had proliferated with every passing year, and how much he had been dreading to put a sign in the window. What were the chances of someone suitable walking in off the street? It was to honor serendipity, therefore, that he made a toast, gulping that first glass down in one. The second Cognac was to pay homage to the loafer that he would never now have to endure, the clumsy meddler he had envisaged coming into his business when he eventually plucked up the courage to put that sign for an assistant in the window. No longer would he need to fear the arrival of that fatuous lout, who would probably never have known a full day's work in their life, and who would almost certainly have burnt his cocoa beans the minute his back was turned, ruining his roasting pots, and causing a fire in his kitchen, becoming the destruction of everything he had built in the process. His second drink, therefore, was to honor the absence of that idler. He raised a glass to their truancy, and prayed to the stars that their paths may never cross. The third Cognac was for the glory of attracting what he sensed he had found. In the army, he was over five kitchen porters.

Many the luddite had been put in his charge, the dopey youth who would grin at him all day as he explained his system, would nod through his instructions without listening to a word he had said. He had come to know the dull-eyed make and shape of a halfwit. Some lapidary stirring of his old gut told him now that this Loulita was not one of them, that by some benevolent force, a practical, quick-witted person of common sense had stepped forth, and found their way into his shop without any effort on his part.

By the fourth Cognac, Helmut had lost the run of his list. But he did form a pact inside his inebriated brain. Despite his good cheer, he would not allow himself to be taken advantage of. Certainly, she might rent the little box of a room above the shop, as she had suggested – it was vacant, so why not? She could stay there but with a proviso. For now, the trainee could live wherever it was that she was living. Helmut would take in no dosser, nor lay about looking for free lodgings. As much as his innards crooned the peaceful ease that signified the arrival of a valuable asset, he would reserve his generosity, and judge her propensity to aid his business on the tangible scale of her actions. Only then might he forget his restraint, and let shine the full rays of generosity.

Chapter 18

September, 1990, Schloss Ludwig

The search for a monumental burial spot for the manuscript caused Tobias Pilzerhoff to upgrade his interest in the estate of Castle Ludwig. Engrossed in didactic endeavors, he thought himself about the flowers, shrubs and plants that shot up here and there, and about the beech trees and pines of its forest. He procured, from the local ordnance survey office, a map of the area. It delineated the land around the castle. With it, he took to inspecting the grounds lot by lot, pushing through thorny bushes, and rummaging about in overgrown corners of dense foliage.

One day, he discovered on his adventures a labyrinth enclosed behind ivy-clad stone. Grappling through a profusion of leaves and moss, he at last heaved himself up on top of its perimeter wall, and from that considerable height perused the dishevelled space, taking in broken pottery, and six rose urns now capsized and abandoned. Launched himself off the wall, he jumped into that hidden void – his Wellingtons making a crisp thud on the rust colored detritus that carpeted its broken concrete floor. Dried leaves had been gusted up into piles, as if some phantom gardener was tending to that forgotten spot, when in fact not one other living human soul had entered that liminal space in more than half a century. Standing up at full height, he surveyed the derelict remains of the flower garden; at its center a fountain. No water came flowing now; the basin cracked, strewn in two parts. The square marble that made up the base was intact, though. It was just about big enough to set a metal box into. Perfect, thought Tobias.

After several weeks of wheelbarrowing, de-weeding, and dead-heading, he started on the trees, pulling out dried carcasses, old trunks and bushes. Then he got to the cutting, pruning and clearing. After that, the place began in earnest to look like what it might have once been. A month into the project, it was time to plant. Then came bone meal fertilizer, and a brush of whitewash for the rose urns. He lifted out the fountain from the center, and after he had done so, he stood back. Left behind was a square crater about two feet deep, precisely the sort of space that he had in mind to bury the manuscript. He measured it with his tape, then stood over it to take account of how it would catch the light. Facing east, it was certainly in keeping with the most ancient of traditions, which suggested that such a direction lent itself to a soul's rise with the sun. If one cared about the classics, delivery into the pearly gates and all that, it was perfect indeed. So it would be here, he affirmed, that the manuscript would rest.

The hardware shop provided him with lead lining, a welding rod, gloves and a helmet mask. It took some time to seal the cube at its corners because it was set in the ground. Inuring himself to the job at hand, and to the awkward angle it required of him, he persevered. When the metal encasing was finished, Tobias waited for the arrival of the flowers. There were still small jobs about the garden to be done, like the tidying up of broken branches, sanding down the bench, the lacquering of a wind indicator arrow designed to swivel to the North or South Pole depending on the weather's direction, a tidy piece of medieval metalwork that had only been revealed when clutches of stubborn ivy were negotiated off. Two days later, the roses came. They were pink, only pink; a dozen boxes of them, freshly cut and driven by lorry all the way from a private grower in Holland. When he had finished laying them, they were packed so tightly into the space that Tobias had to stamp them down in order to make them fit. As he leaned forward, and placed the manuscript in the center of the flower pit, their sudden scent hit his nostrils. It caused his pupils to dilate, and then his eyes to close involuntarily, and his senses to pull at the choral notes of that concentrated aroma made up of one million delicately scented rose petals.

With one hand hung over that pink floral ocean, Tobias suspended, found himself then in limbo. Unable to commit to keeping that parchment, or letting it go, he stood for some time in that inane position, peering into the pit, his hand grasping the manuscript, his diaphragm expanding to its full capacity feeding greedily on the rose petals perfume for all he was worth.

He understood at last what it was all about, this writing that pulled at the souls of some but not others. He knew that the sensory paradise that the author had attempted to convey in words were the very words that she had been deprived of in that charnel house, and he knew the reason for the strength and power of her words was down to the place within her from which they came. Her words came out of unwavering purity, of turning herself to light in the darkest possible circumstances. She had not written this book because she had wanted to, like he did, to reach his ego's summit, or to make himself known or remembered, or adored, or anything else. She had written it because she had not been able to stop herself from writing. Then he let it go; let her go. As her parchment fell towards the earth, a gust caught the booklet so that in its final resting position, it was open at the page of a Yiddish Prayer. It took some time to pull his eyes off that page of Chets and Tavs. So overcome was he that he read it several times to himself, then said it aloud. It was so solemn, so final that eventually his eyes glassed up, and he allowed himself to release from them some tears. There was no one around to witness him doing it – save for three sparrows, a Robin and a balled up hedgehog sleeping in an unseen hole at the base of a tree. Sealing the tomb would have to wait for another day, such was the overwhelming grief which caused him to be depleted by contemplation on the cruelty of life at the stark sight of that little grave. That plot made her real. Her life had been so short, the living time robbed, and yet so much had come out of that life. He had become a part of it, perhaps. At least her words had survived, due in part to his doing, even if no one knew her name. So he let those roses sit in the open air until the next evening, their perfume soaking into the paper, and returned after dark to begin welding. Making it airtight took the entire night; blue and white sparks crackling, spitting furious fits of incandescence at an angular helmet with a slot of glass for his eyes. By dawn, it was done. He put his hands together, bent his head, closed his eyes, and whispered 'Goodbye,' then pushed the covering flagstone over the metal case, and stood back. But something was amiss.

The concrete was clinically bare, coldly new against the crumbling glory of the old flower garden. It was too clean, the type of clean that signposted a disturbance. That was not what Tobias had been aiming for. This was meant to be a discreet burial place. But now, anyone who came, as unlikely as that may be, would notice its blatant freshness. It looked too much like what it was: a grave. What was needed, he decided, was a centerpiece, a sculpture that would draw the eye away from the base altogether. It would also serve to mark this as the place where The Scent of Heaven finally came to rest, known only to him.

Tobias turned around, and walked towards the gate. It groaned begrudgingly. Then it sulked to a stop, wedged itself stuck, leaving not enough room for him to squeeze through. He tugged at it, but it refused to negotiate, as if some force held it fast. A force that wanted to keep him there, to stay with the project because his work wasn't done. 'Alright, alright, but not today,' he said aloud, dispatching a fulsome and almighty kick thereafter, which caused the gate to swing loose, spinning around its hinge with a bewailing squeal. Walking back towards the castle, Tobias could see the headlights of cars moving along the Autobahn. They came through a haze, a morning dew that had sunk down the mountain during the night, settling on the valley below. Watching the traffic, he considered those people heading to office jobs in the city now; off to Düsseldorf, he supposed, to work in real estate, or department stores, or law firms, offices, shops, or hospitals to do whatever it was that people did when they went to work.

People did that. He knew it, of course. People worked in jobs with bosses, got paid by the hour, took on chores they didn't like for the money, to pay bills. It was a fact of life for many, but he had never done it himself. He was a writer, and the son of a writer. His job was to come up with stories, ones that people wanted to read, and to write them down in a way that people found pleasantly absorbing. Blossoms, his next book, would be like that. It would be his greatest achievement because he understood now what his writing had to be about. It had to come from the truest part of him, and from that place alone. Now that he had paid his karmic dues, he would find the words for a narrative epic that would make people want to read it, people like the ones travelling in their cars along the motorway below. He would waste no time, and start his masterpiece today. Once inside the castle, Tobias pulled a chair up to his desk, and looked at the screen of his computer. He rubbed his hands together, placing them over the keyboard with expectant zeal. Now that he had put The Scent of Heaven ceremoniously to rest, and was a global name; now that he was a highly regarded and established writer, Blossoms could be born. It was a fine title, if he did say so himself. A good start. Surely, that title would carry him to the midheaven of his career, to its highest point, a moment when inspiration would flow his way. He stared at the screen, but the cursor only jeered and blinked back at him as before. That's OK, he told himself and shrugged to relieve the tension mounting between his scapula, rotating his head around to relieve the pain brewing.

A slow start was to be expected. There had been a lull in his writing, and he could not propose to jump straight into a novel; not at least one of the caliber of which Blossoms would be. There should be a period of easing into it. With that, he closed his eyes and took in a breath, during which he tried to visualize the word Blossoms in his mind, but all he saw was the manuscript sitting atop all those pink flowers. Another attempt along the same line brought only the overwhelming memory of those final notes of rose, that engulfing fusion of heavenly scent. Aside from reoccurring evocations of the rose garden, and the secrets enclosed there, nothing much happened at all. He tried one more time, but the result was the same. Then he slouched in his chair. He had worn the writer's costume, played the part, had his name and face printed on every newspaper, had been nominated for the biggest book prizes in Europe and beyond, and yet he still had not written, and could not write a single thing of note. All was lost, and yet to the waiting world beyond this room, he was as decorated as any heroic man of vision. The more he thought of it, the more the irony tickled him, and from some maniacal place of illogical rule, he began to laugh. With head thrown back, he roared out loud, then folding himself forward over that roar of irony until it became one of hopeless grief, he began to sob.

Holding his face in his hands, his shoulders bobbed under the weight of a lifetime of disillusionment. Here sat a fool, a schlemiel, a cuckold, a man bewildered by his own false image, a decade's worth of self-deceit. Here was a man who had held onto a fruitless dream for too long to let go of it now because without it, there was no 'him'. Who was this Tobias Pilzerhoff, who stared back at him in the morning when he splashed water on his face, if not the striver, the trier, the man of limitless forbearance and patience beyond the humane in search of his great book? He had only ever been that. Those were the built elements of him, the foundations that he had depended on to be himself. Now a trapdoor had been pulled beneath him, the mathematics that made up reason had not added up in the final calculation. The equation hadn't worked out. It had turned out that his life did not add up, his existence had been proven to be false, to be leading him to a nonsensical calculus, a meaningless nothingness. There was no hope. It was over. For three days, he moped about the castle, taking each night a bottle down to the rose garden where he sat drinking, and lamenting, sometimes shouting, and finally crying into the stone slab in the center. By midnight of his third spree, he was lying down on his back, studying the sky. Watching the panorama of infinite, opalescent planets voyaging overhead, seeing that expanse of navy and countless pins of silver, he forgot his misery, and began instead to count the stars, reciting over and over an old German children's tale.

It was the story of a boy who wanted to write, but having been careless about his step, that boy had walked into a river and had been carried away. Although the boy was saved, his beloved writing book was lost in the deluge, and the schemata of his life plan floated past him, gone in a split second of

nascent chance.

'Die Geschichte von Hans Guck-in-die-Luft 'Guck-in-die-Luft, Guck-in-die-Luft,

Guck-in-dieLuft….'

Chapter 19

October, 1990, Brussels

Helmut had been right about Loulita Hirsch. From the very first morning that she arrived, Loulita's apprenticeship

at Müllers Palais de Praliné showed her to be an impeccable trainee. She had arrived on time, and with an open face had listened to all that Helmut had to tell her. One of the first chocolate making facts she learned was that fermented dried cocoa beans were ordered from the wholesaler as needed, and that the sensitive kidney shaped seeds that arrived in a sack could not be stored on the premises for long, lest they soak up other cooking odors from the kitchen, or even moisture from the air. Such elementals could be the wastage of an entire sack; and waste, Loulita was told, was something that Helmut did not abide. She nodded her head, taking in each command without question.

They moved on, and Helmut showed her next the device for cleaning the beans, and demonstrated how to vacuum away dried cocoa pulp, wood, fibers, sand and pieces of the pod kernel. Then he showed her how to weigh and blend to his specifications, and how to heat the roasting oven above 107 degrees Celsius. When he poured out the beans, Helmut turned his back so that she would not learn his secret mix;

a nine-bean blend, the one that gave Müllers Palais de Praliné chocolate its unique sweet, nutty flavor. It would not have meant anything to her, but he had forgotten that there were people in the world who didn't spend their mind on such things. Next, she was indoctrinated into the workings of the winnowing machine where beans crackled and baked under serrated cones, a fan then blowing the superfluous remnants away so that only the soft, naked nib of the cocoa bean was left behind.

'Come and see how the ground nibs look once they have been filtered and purified and the cocoa removed. The butter is the essential component of high-quality Belgian chocolate. Looks just like ordinary table butter from a cow, doesn't it?' Loulita nodded. 'And it is just like that, only it is much more special. It is this cocoa butter that adds luster and delicate glaze to all pralines and truffles,' said Helmut, standing tall over his gleaming trays. Such were the details that Loulita acquired from Helmut during those initial weeks. One day, her new boss turned towards the oven. 'Now for something extraordinary,' he said. Directing Loulita to follow him, he drew her eye to the rich brown beans cooking underneath a yellow flame, and told her to breathe the smell in. And there it was, the undeniable, unforgettable first inhalation of fresh melted Belgian chocolate, a fragrance that would never leave her, and would become, in her memory, the marker for this period of her life.

'The roasting stage is where the flavor of the chocolate is formed. It is most important.'

'What time should I give to roasting?'

'When you are ready to roast cocoa beans by yourself, my dear, you will not go by the clock on the wall but by your God-given senses. Until that time, I will do it. Now we must clean and sterilize, and return each item to its rightful place before we leave. In my kitchen, everything has a place.'

Loulita extended her time at the lodgings on the Grand Palace until Helmut handed her the key to the upstairs pad.

It was a furtherance of just four weeks.

After the old box room was cleared, the crates taken way, and the floorboards scrubbed and varnished, and the old brick fireplace cleared of crows nests, she moved in. The bed was on a mezzanine on stilts above the sofa. It was just a mattress, really, so high up that a ladder was needed to get on it. Sitting underneath that structure, reading a book was her new diversion.

Perhaps it was that Belgian city air, infused so faintly with chocolate, sugar, vanilla and almonds, or maybe it was down to the novel she had started reading that night; the story of a young girl's Homeric journey to find the most blissful smells on earth. Whatever it was, she was not scared, or one bit nervous about some intruder breaking in, or about waking up to find a shadowy figure at the end of her bed, or of being alone in that little flat. Because of this lack of fear, she did something that she never usually did; she reached over to the little bedside locker and switched out the light.

Then the shallow lines in her forehead softened, her small, darting eyes became still, and her peaky ears stopped listening for sounds of imminent danger. Being encapsulated within the protective alms of her new nest had brought forth a sense of such comforting singularity that she might have been a shrew who had burrowed deep into the ground to find a perfect place to fit its own form, as the world went on above. For Loulita, the taxi had started out as a way of being free. To her sister's horror, she had used what money came from her parents' accident to buy her license outright. Between passengers, Loulita used to dream about old buildings and hidden alleyways, but above all about the cryptic behavior of the human beings that she came across in her car, like the man taking leave to meet his mistress, or the wife surreptitiously crossing town to make a lodgement into her escape fund, the gambler on a lunchtime flutter, the pastor on a drinking spree, the medical student in a bra and miniskirt, the married man who paid her fare home. The taxi had brought her up close to all these stories. It had often brought her too close, and required on more than one occasion for her to shout, and fight to get the fees she was due. She could not defend herself, not physically anyway, and so she had used her imagination to save her, had become someone else within those times using coarse language, and spitting on her own floor in the hope that this rough demeanor would act as a decoy. It must have worked because when she evoked this lewd persona, narrowed eyes detached themselves from her, and catastrophe was averted. Still she considered it only a matter of time until the day or night came when she would not see that assailant coming. Then what? Those concerns were behind her now that she had found a new way to earn her keep, in a new city where nobody knew her past, or cared. There were indeed much more favorable places and jobs, but not for her. This new life was as good as any she could have hoped for. What were the chances of finding a pleasant occupation, and quaint lodgings in Brussels, a location she would never have considered before now?

In her mind, Belgium's capital had always been a banal place, all fatty chips and frothy beer. What would one do in a city whose national emblem was a boy relieving himself in a fountain? But now that she had become acquainted with the undercurrent of light-hearted humor, she understood that city's' deeper character, recognized the intelligence of the place. Its philosophy was based, she supposed, on the recognition that life is just too short and precious to be taken so seriously all the time. Few places are smart enough to laugh at life as Brussels could. That city's comic peppered psyche was evident all around, in its art, its theatre, its people. There was only one way to say it; Brussels was fun. Now, if she could have hermetically sealed herself off from the world, and stayed in that place, and lived out her life in that city, she would have. Here, she could read and dream and stare into space and write and occasionally go out and walk, or – when the mood took her – run along the river, or thread though avenues, squares, streets, allowing small lanes to reveal themselves gradually, and take her where they might. Her new boss was pleasing, even though he constantly tried to feed her chocolate.

'Oh no, thanks,' said Loulita, on the first day that Helmut handed her a cup of hot cocoa.

'I don't drink that.'

'You don't drink chocolate?' Helmut stood before her staring in disbelief. This was the first time he had really looked at her as anything other than his new assistant, and what he saw now caused him to raise one eyebrow. There was no meat on her bones at all.

'You must have something in your stomach to keep you going if you are to work. I insist upon it.' Loulita liked living alone. There was nobody to comment on what she did or didn't do, or to notice what she put into her mouth, or how thin she was. Only he had noticed, despite the thick woolen jumpers she wore under the white cooking coat.

'I never take breakfast,' said Loulita. Helmut huffed, putting the cup down beside her. 'Take it. It will do you good,' he said, walking away back towards the heated oven, where he began using a small stainless-steel scoop to shovel the beans into it. Pouring the chocolate down the sink, she distracted him with a question. 'Is this the only way to roast beans?'

'The only way?' he said immediately, engrossed again in the craft. 'Of course this is not the only way,' he boomed. There were, she learned that day because she wanted to avoid eating and so redirected the conversation, no less than five ways to roast cocoa. Oven roasting was best, Helmut said because he felt that things should be done according to age- old artisan chocolate craftsmanship.

'The basic technique for roasting cocoa beans does not change no matter the process,' said Helmut, the oven's golden light showering his face in warm ochre. He watched her as he spoke, noticing now her legs and arms, how brittle they were. As he talked, he considered that maybe she was naturally composed this way, as some people are. Stick-like, no matter how much they consume, they remain as slight as a lat, as rickety thin as the bistro chair by the door on which she sat.

'The idea is to bring the beans to a high temperature at first, then reduce it slowly.'

'How do you know when to turn the heat down?' asked Loulita, firing questions as decoys. He knew what she was doing, of course, and her efforts to deflect from the food he had offered made him understand just how high the defence walls around her were. It confirmed what he had thought originally, told him that what she had shown of herself before was merely a shallow veil worn by someone who didn't like herself, or rather didn't yet know the real person that lived within.

'You must do that when the beans first begin cracking, and well before they start to burn.' Loulita looked at the beans in the furnace.

'Can you see them cracking?' asked Helmut. 'No. I don't believe I can, but I can hear them.'

'Very good. Sehr schön! This job is always better done when one consults their ears. You will hear them pop. That happens when they get to around 120 Celsius. Listen.'

137

Helmut put his head to one side, and Loulita did the same. With the heat of the fire warming their faces, they stood in silence, listening to the sound made by water vapor exploding from the heated seeds, both of them avoiding the real conversation, the one hidden now just below the surface.

'What happens after that?' asked Loulita.

'Then they are done. You can pick one up and taste it,' said Helmut. Taking a hot bean up with a small tong, he gesticulated for Loulita to do the same.

'Be careful now. Don't burn your mouth,' he said, watching her bring it to her face. She did as he said, and incised the powdery bean.

'What do you taste?'

'Chocolate,' she answered. Moving her hand to put the rest of the hot bean down on the counter, Helmut took her hand and stopped it midway.

'Go ahead, you can eat it.'

'Oh no, that's OK. I won't,' said Loulita.

'It's only one cocoa bean.' Irritated, she spat out the piece into her hand and looked at him, defiant eyes trained on his.

'No, thanks.' He held her gaze, raised his bushy eyebrows. She stared back, then pulled her hand away. Shocked by this defensive struggle, he turned back to his teaching.

'It tastes like chocolate?' She nodded. 'Then, it is ready.'

'I see,' she smiled resuming control thinking what a relief it was that he had moved on and not held onto that awkward confrontation about her in-take of food. She liked him, and did not want to offend him. She liked the way he did not care to rid himself of the patois that gave away his humble beginnings. She liked the boundary that still existed between him and her, and she wanted to keep it in place. He was definitely from the north, Strasbourg, she would have guessed. He wasn't concerned with grammar, but instead used language as a functional message, caring only about the core communication; about what was being conveyed. His way of speaking, the insouciant lack of pretentiousness, was something to value. Listening to him was music to the ears, if only he would move off from this fixation with her nutrition so that their companionship as worker and assistant could proceed. But Helmut Englehaus didn't have it in him to leave things under the ground. He was one of those who dredged for reality, no matter the cost. His soul demanded it of him. He was a digger, a burrower, one whose purpose it was to drill deep and bring up – in all its unembellished queerness and nudity – the truth.

People are always fixated on something, thought Loulita. At university, there was a fixation with precision, an over-concern with being right, leading to pointless arguments to do with language or books. All of that called her to value the purity of those who didn't spend their lives thinking of their next sentence. She had met too many spoofers, humble- braggers bent on presenting themselves always in the best light whilst feigning modesty, and cracking any opportunity at underhand one-upmanship. It was irksome, tedious after a while. He wasn't like that. He was a straight talker, only perhaps too straight.

'The most important instrument you have in making chocolate is your nose,' Helmut broke into her thoughts, his voice taking her back to the task at hand.

'Concentrate,' he continued, tapping one finger at the side of his balding head. Then, he wafted smoke from the oven with the same hand, and moved his head into it, sniffing the patch of steam, motioning for her to do the same.

'Come, you will smell heaven now.' She did as she was told, and as she inhaled, a wave of pleasure came over her so profound that it showed in her eyes. Helmut recognized it. 'You got the smell? Huh? Good?'

'Yes, very good indeed,' said Loulita.

'When they emit this toasty aroma, they are done. If you smell the burning, you have gone too far. The batch is spoiled, and you must then start over. Again, what do you smell, Fräulein?' he asked one more time.

'I smell chocolate,' said Loulita. 'Right again. Good. Yes. Schön. We are getting somewhere.'

Loulita smiled at his infectious passion.

'It is a simple goal. We are making chocolate, so when we get the smell of chocolate, we are on the right track. We are not making burnt things, so when we get the smell of burnt things, we are going wrong. Makes sense? Easy peasy?' Loulita nodded.

'Always remember to listen to the senses,' said Helmut, tapping several more times on his own hooked proboscis.

'The nose. The eyes, and something of the instinct. We practice with these instruments everywhere we go, do you get it now?' Loulita nodded.

'Tomorrow, you will come in before me and have the oven ready, yes?'

'Yes, I will,' said Loulita.

Chapter 20

November, 1990, Brussels

Loulita had by now well and truly made the apartment above the shop her own. At first, she did miss the view of the medieval market square below, and the lit-up guild houses of Brussels, whose craftsmen had soared to the status of nobility through dedication to their guilds. Every artisan had a saint in Brussels, a guide to ask for protection. The butchers, fishmongers, greengrocers, sawyers, goldsmiths and silversmiths had Our Lady of the Lake. The weavers, bleachers, fullers, hatters, tapestry makers and linen weavers had St. Lawrence. St. John was for the blacksmiths, the tinsmiths, farriers, pan smiths, cutlers, locksmiths and watchmakers, and St Luke for the painters, gold-beaters, glassmakers, the saddlers, the harness makers, the turners, plasterers, stuccadores, thatcher's and basket weavers. With so many saints around, she thought, no wonder the buildings here were of such high quality and exquisite finish.

She had studied, during her nights at the hostel, the lit effigies of each guild's patron saint blazing down from the various facades, had moved her eye towards the glimmering lights of the Town Hall; that most magnificent of buildings.

It had seen as much tragedy as honor; a make-shift hospital during the first world war, later taken over by Nazis when the second war came.

Snapping herself away from her former residence, Loulita pulled the battered suitcase towards the wardrobe. Now that she had fully moved into her new lodgings, she was going to put it away. It was easy to lift because it was empty, except for the box that her aunty had left her in her will. As she squeezed the case into the narrow closet, she realized too late that it was not properly zipped up. Out tumbled the box of letters, its contents landing in a pile before her, dozens of handwritten pages and stamped envelopes from a girl called Anne addressed to her aunty Kitty. On top was the padded brown envelope from Christie's Auction House, London. The package was addressed to the hostel in Berlin where she had been staying at the time that she had gotten the idea to send her aunt's letters to Christies for valuation, in the hope of extrapolating relevance from the pile strewn now at her feet. Who was this girl called Anne?

Packing those letters off to Christie's was all she could think to do with them, since she had no idea why her aunty had gone to the trouble of leaving this box of oddities to her in her last will and testimony. Why did she bother? It was just a pile of useless junk; old letters from the war between her aunty and a childhood pen pal, someone she had never met, and never would because they were all dead by now. A fat lot of good such sentimentalities were to her, a pack of letters between a pack of dead people. In a way, she wished they had been lost in the post on the way back from Christie's in London. Perhaps that is why she had sent them away. If they had been lost, she would not have had to think about them now. But they had found their way back to her someone, and here they were again causing vexation, making her wonder about the meaning of this unruly pile at her feet.

It made her blush now when she remembered that she had genuinely believed that her aunty Kitty had been the pen pal of Anne Frank, just because the girl who wrote to aunty Kitty was Jewish, lived in Amsterdam and was called Anne. She couldn't help it. Her nature was to dream up links, to visualize how incidents may be connected by fine threads. It was why her writing flowed so well. Only that such a buoyant creative mind hadn't proven particularly helpful in other aspects of ordinary everyday living. A teeming imagination is such a useless skill, she thought, unless one happens to be a plutocratic heiress, which she wasn't. What must they have thought in Christie's Auction House? Another nutcase fixated on some old letters; another war fanatic making up outlandish claims. They probably got eccentrics writing to them all the time. It consoled her to think of all the strange items that must get pushed through that polished brass London letter box, and her boundless imagination set to carry her away again, only that she interrupted it by bending down to pick up one of the letters at her feet, and read it over. Then she laid it on the floor, and tipped out the rest of the notes and envelopes from the box.

At the base of the container was a layer of crinkled pink tissue paper. She pulled it up, expecting to find nothing but white cardboard underneath. But there was something else, more letters in different writing, and some old photographs too.

New York, 1942 Lieber Samuel,

I have missed you very much since we last met in Frankfurt. I hope it is OK to write that in a letter, my darling. It has been many years, I know, but I have thought about you often. Germany is too dangerous now, and so I have come to New York to stay with relatives. Claude would not leave. These are terrifying times.

How is your wife? I remember that you talked of coming to New York. I enclose my address overleaf.

Deine, Ingrid

*****

New York, 1953 Lieber Samuel,

145

It was wonderful to see you in Manhattan. If only things were different, but there are others to think about. The things you said will stay with me, and I have the same feelings for you. But life is as it is.

Deine, Ingrid

New York, 1960 Lieber Samuel,

I was so happy to hear that you will travel to New York in the spring. There are some lovely bookshops that you will enjoy looking around. I might go with you to pick up a gift for Claude. His latest book has been a big success. Its promotion takes my husband travelling all across America.

He will be in the south as part of a tour of the states at that time. I wanted to go with him, but he prefers to be alone.

We tried for a baby, but it seems God has decided family is not for us. This makes Claude very sad. It is a lot for him to remember, and talk to audiences about all the terrible events that he witnessed in Frankfurt. He has suffered. A child would distract him from the past.

Looking forward to seeing you soon.

Deine, Ingrid

*****

New York, 1960, December Lieber Samuel,

A child was born a few weeks ago here in Frankfurt, a strong, healthy boy.

For the boy's and for Claudes sake, I urge you to let us go. Claude is happy believing what he believes. He does not need to know the truth.

I know that you will understand. We have named the boy Tobias.

Deine, Ingrid

*****

Loulita looked at the three photographs in the box. The first was of her father Samuel Hirsch with her mother, who had both died so young in a tragic car accident. The second photograph, also black and white, showed her mother standing in front of an old-fashioned car with children – two little girls. That was her and her sister, she supposed.

The third photograph was more recent, its color faded. It showed a different woman, one with Nordic blonde hair and twinkling navy-blue eyes. She was dressed in a miniskirt, and was smiling at the camera, a baby in her arms. Loulita turned the picture over. Ingrid and Tobias, 1960. She didn't know them.

Chapter 21

May, 1991, Brussels

Müllers Palais de Praliné profited from the addition of its new worker, and time was now a luxury for Loulita.

It was not about the workload. The making of chocolate brought up a need for precision and order, persuasions that caused her to worry; to get stuck in details, to run lists and stock sheets through her head at night. Had that delivery of cocoa beans come in today? Such racing thoughts meant that her body seldom achieved slumber before midnight.

During those months, she opened aunty Kitty's box of letters many times, and read the words over and over. Why had her aunty left her these things? What did they mean? Kitty had been her father's sister, had become her guardian after the accident. Her father wanted her to have these letters, but why? She would never know, just as she would never know who this woman was that her father had written to. They were having, it seemed, some illicit affair, him and this woman Ingrid, behind her mother's back during the war. What bearing did that have on her? It was a cruel joke to set her up with more obfuscations, as if there were not enough already. Samuel and Kitty were dead, and she was on her own. Those letters only proved that her father was a cad, that her parents didn't love each other, and that marriages were rarely all they are made out to be – like she needed to get that sort of confirmation left to her in a will. On occasions that she found herself liberated from her work, and energized enough to do so, she took a jaunt out of town. Today, Loulita packed a book into her rucksack, and went to the garage where her taxi was parked. She pulled the plastic sheet back, sat in, and drove for one hour and twenty minutes south of Brussels to the quaint medieval town of Dinart to walk down to Rocher Bayard, a rock formation that sliced up the heavens. Summer had come so fast that Loulita had hardly noticed it happening. When she reached the path that led off the main road, she couldn't find the entrance to the track. The gap in the hedge that brought walkers off the concrete and into the thick of nature was now a deluge of thorny bushes. Even when she reached the spot where she knew the entrance to the hiking trail was supposed to be, it was so overgrown with fronds of green that she had to prod against the bristly growth with a stick in order to find the least dense part. When at last she established the track, and started down it, the briars brushed against her hands, clawing seeds leaving fragments of dried, amputated fauna on her clothes; advancing her arms over her head to stop herself from being scratched and stung by thorns and waist-high nettles, she walked.

A few meters on, the path flattened out, and the misty aluminium expanse of river water came into view. As always, the sight of it made her breathe out. It caused her worries to disappear, replaced with the soothing reggae pace that leaked sporadically out from behind messy bushes of thorn or bramble, a sound that gave away libertines, teenagers mostly, who came out to Diant at the weekend from the city to drink bottles of beer. They didn't wander too far down the path. A kilometer would be far enough for them to be out of sight and earshot. Anywhere on the path after that, and she would be alone. She glanced over at the familiar cliff face, its crenulations of grey and black stone just a haze now because of a misty hew that hung around the rock, and seeped out halfway across the river obscuring its details, making ghost-ships of passing boats moving through the water.

Along the path she went, taking into her nostrils notes of devil's bread, yellow gorse and white garlic flower, fragrances that appeared, interchanged and faded with each step. At a small in-cove, the gravelly way opened onto a scree stone pebble beach where people waded at the edge of the river in bathing suits. Moving on, the path became steep as she negotiated her way up flag-stone steps. She extended her hand, and felt about for the first of the three

151

pyramids, a man-made handle carved into the cliff as a grip to steady hikers. Now she could just about see the bald geometric terrain of hills, as well as the cold stone bridge coming up ahead. Once on the far side of the bridge, she would find protective solitude.

Hiking on through a field with sporadic boulders, passing a mossy stone jagged-topped wall that fizzled out turning into random posts strung together with brown, rusted barbwire and the odd nail, she pushed on, concentrating on her breath. Once again, hedges raged green on both sides every step of the way. As the path narrowed, emerald velvet ferns and purple topped thistles rocketed over low prickly nettles. She rounded the last corner and saw her place, the hidden patch at the end of the bridge. Pulling the backpack off her shoulders when she reached it, Loulita dropped to the ground, and let her body be enveloped in a blanket of mauve, yellow and white speckled meadow grass.

It felt good to let her bones settle on the springy ground, like going back into the earth before one's time. Beside her now, a brook rushed urgently over mossy green rocks. It ran towards the river, destined in time to meet silted shores, and then at last find freedom in the sea. The wind whistled in the distance, roiling against the cliffs, augmenting the screaming laments of seabirds who circled overhead. A modest truck rattling over the motorway returned as a juggernaut, exaggerated acoustics making it like the hammer of phantom panel beaters, working furiously to build something high in the rocky summit, up there with the gulls. In the grassy meadow sanctuary, bees came and went. A peaceful breeze shifted the heath. An airplane left a contrail of white on the warm blue sky above her head. Birds tweeted and charmed the day away as she lay, head resting on her folded sweater. Laid out prone, eyes closed, she gripped a thick stalk of grass, and twirled it idly between her fingers, then opened the book over her face, and began to read; The Scent of Heaven by Tobias Pilzerhoff.

Time passed – two hours, maybe more. Loulita was easily a quarter way through the book now. Then she closed her eyes, and was back in the museum in Berlin reading a letter encapsulated inside a Perspex box. Dozing, her mind's eye caught sight of a seagull flying overhead. She blinked. Way, way out it went over the river, then back towards the rocks, over an expanse of never-ending water, taking her with it on a dream. Eyelids resting, she was back in Berlin again. Through a seagull's vision, she panned the city below, hovering above the grounds of The Jewish Museum, saw that disjointed star that made up its brutal form; the hypothesis coming to her causing her eyes to flicker. It was just too outlandish

to entertain, even by her standards; that the letters – the ones her aunt had left her, and the writing in this novel The Scent of Heaven - had been done by the same person. What she was thinking did not make sense. It was the sleight of a febrile psyche, she told herself, a mind attempting to join up the dots to create a more fitting narrative existence than the patchy one doled out to her. Why had this book become so enmeshed in her brain? She thought for a moment, then settled on an answer. Her wild imagination had come to demand its pound of flesh, to press her to start writing again. That was it, but why was she so stuck on this novel? Why this book? Could it be simply that she had not been expressing that ethereal, illogical side of herself, had not been honoring that powerful imagination or hers, because she had become too busy to commit herself to it, had gotten engaged in practical endeavors - kitchen supplies - had gotten bogged down in the here and now of life?

That would explain this outpouring, this juxtaposition that kept presenting itself to her tangled up subconscious with elemental fragments of her own reality, a pastiche fused of the make believe and the actual. It was ridiculous. Moreover, it was impossible. It could not be true. How could it? This book, The Scent of Heaven that she was reading had only just been published. It said Pilzerhoff in a large serif font below the title. Tobias Pilzerhoff. She had seen him on TV, and remembered meeting him once at a night-class back in Frankfurt, before he had risen to fame. On campus, Loulita's peers had joked about her odd knack of being able to decipher Dostoevsky from Tolstoy, Gogol from Chekhov, Joyce from Borges. It was the one thing about her they seemed to find unanimously laudable, amused that you could read out one sentence to her, then put five books before her; that if she had read any of them before, even in part, she never got it wrong. In one line she could identify the writer, and not alone that but very often, could describe the context, such was her ability to memorize and absorb, and recognize an author from a fragment of their work, after having tasted just a tiny slither, a minute sample of prose. If they ever come up with a Booker for literary parlor games, you'll be nominated for sure, old bean.

Loulita couldn't explain it exactly, could only say that writing styles were for her as unique as the ridges and lines on a person's fingers. Never more certain had she been than she was now that this book had been written by the same hand that had penned the letters that she had in her possession; the letters from Anne to her aunty Kitty postmarked during the war. Wide awake and fully alert now, Loulita sat up, shook away her doze, got to her feet, and stood firm on corporeal ground, staring at her watch. A lone ant crawled up a blade of bending grass. Considering, she watched it. Then, brushing the detritus from her clothes, she darted back through the scraggly bushes, running over the flagstone steps to where the pyramid carvings aided a walker's grip. Down she went by the scree beach, passing bathers, and a yapping dog chasing a red Frisbee.

Two hours later she was back in Brussels, had dug out five letters from the old suitcase, and was sitting on the floor underneath the mezzanine bed; the book opened, the letters strewn around. Whoever had written the letters left by aunty Kitty was one and the same person as the one who had written that book, The Scent of Heaven.

Chapter 22

May, 1991, Brussels

Hello, Hello. Is that the roasting of my oven that I smell?'
said Helmut, closing the front door of Müllers Palais de
Praliné behind him.

'Yes. It is at nearly thirty seven degrees Celsius now.'
'Excellent. I will make a fine chocolatier of you one day.'
He began, as he always did, by making the morning brew,

and handed Loulita a mug of thick hot cocoa. As always,
she took it, as if she intended to drink it.

'What is the best bean in your opinion?' she asked, turning
her head to look for a ledge near the sink to tip the liquid
away when he was distracted. But Helmut did not answer.
He raised an eye-brow, and the smile fell from his face.

'You are not hungry?' he said, lowering his chin, meeting
her eyes with the full intensity of his own. 'You must have
something to keep you going,' he added. She put the cup to
her nose, closed her eyes, let herself experience the sweet
smell, and felt her mouth fill up with water from it. Her
tummy gave a longing yearn. He lowered his head and
peered at her. She lowered her own to the plump dark rose-
brown liquid, watching the hypnotic swirls of full thick

cream rotate. It was her choice to drink it or not. She was the one who decided.

'Are you ready to start roasting?' she said, not meeting his gaze because she knew it would not work this time.

'You cannot keep going like this,' he said.

But still, she did not look up, and felt a twinge in her throat, a familiar sharp bite, as she made the decision to deny herself the tiniest sip of the food which could take the pangs of hunger in her stomach away. The dizziness was the worst, the cloudy haze that fugued her mind out of starvation. It came on without warning, like vertigo. Sometimes it was so overwhelming that she thought she might faint. That was the inconvenient thing about not eating enough, the sudden blacking out and falling over. 'You can take a little,' he said. She ignored him and continued to smell the contents of the cup.

'I'm not hungry, that's all,' Loulita said with a frail smile. If she drank hot chocolate, and let her guard down, what would happen when something chaotic and unexpected came at her again? A phone call from Frankfurt, perhaps, informing her that someone else had died, maybe her sister this time, or one of the children. Something random and cruelly improbable, like the news that both your parents had been killed in a car crash, or something even worse – so bad that she could not even imagine it. Readiness was what was needed to take the sting out of it next time because the shock was half the devastation. She had to stay pepped for when the merciless hand of arbitrary havoc found her, as it had every time she thought she had found her footing. Helmut moved away, began to work on something or other in the back scullery. Every time she had found something stable to cling to, it had not lasted. Someone or something had always come at her. She thought about university, about the bullying, the surreptitious emails, the jeering looks, the trolling, how the tutors had blamed it on her, made it about her age, and turned a blind eye. They had laughed at her. 'People in their forties don't get bullied. That is only for the naive, young student, for the ingénue. Surely, you know how to handle yourself by now,' they had said. And 'what have you done to upset your classmates?' She hadn't upset them, had not meant to anyway. The bullies were made up of a cohort of just three students in fact. She could have ignored them, but once again, it had been her fault. That was the part that was unfair. What she didn't understand was why anyone would want to become a writer so desperately when they only tolerated space in their heads for someone else's theories, and ideas, standard ones. Maybe, they had sensed her dismay at the pretentious babble that came from them. Out of nowhere one of them would shout 'hypocrite' when she was speaking or make some other ill-fitting, out of context comment that would only make sense if one happened to be privvy to the subtext, the background gossip going on between them in private. On one occasion, they read out a poem about a thin old woman going through menopause. She saw them giggling, side-eyeing one another, nodding her way.

'At your age, it's expected that younger students will challenge you. I'm sure you can handle it.' At your age. That's what she had been told when she had reported them. What had she been thinking in making a complaint? Those three had parents who could buy and sell the professors with donations to the faculty, and very likely did judging by the reactions of denial she had encountered.

Of all the 'isms', agism seemed to be the one that didn't count, because there was no society fighting against it on the campus, perhaps, as there was for other societal forms of discrimination. Was it that people only cared if there was something in it for them, some badge that they could award themselves to say they did the 'good thing', and were therefore the 'good person.' If no-one was watching, did no-one care? It seemed that way to her. When she left university, no one even bothered to enquire as to why.

Now Helmut wanted her to drink chocolate. Why? There was no-one watching to say he did a good thing; that he saved his anorexic employee. What was it to him if she did or didn't eat, if she went hungry or not? That wasn't his business. His business was to pay her and hers was to do her job. And she had done that. It wasn't fair. What did he want with trying to make her take food she didn't choose to take? Would he sack her, throw her out if she didn't comply? He was probably secretly interviewing someone else at this very time; someone who would take her place once he had found an opportunity to take her aside and say 'Sorry, but this isn't working.' Then she would have to leave, go back to where she belonged, roaming the world alone.

Why was it that people always overstepped the mark? They came slowly at first so that you hardly noticed, and then one day, they were shouting into your face, or humiliating you in some other less tangible way that was hard to describe, backing each other up to make you look asinine, outdated, or politically incorrect. Nobody would stand up for you, or had tried to help before, too scared to bring the bullies on themselves, or to get inveigled into a maelstrom. That is how people are, she thought. They only care when there is something in it for them. So, what did he want? Or had he just turned against her, grown tired of her, wanted to replace her, and was therefore trying to find a reason to dismiss her?

People always turned against you in the end. A darkness would appear in their eyes at some point. They would start to watch, hone in, see that you were awkward, socially unacclimated, had no-one to back you up, and start to take a little too much notice. Then they would charge. It was about then that she usually decided to move on. She supposed she would be moving on from Brussels soon too, now that he had started on at her with these quips about her eating.

Nobody would help. People didn't help when you lost your way. Why would they? What was in it for them? She was middle-aged with no family, no husband, and nobody by her side. Who was there to care? Her sister had given up on her, thought she was crazy for buying a taxi with the money she had received after their parents' accident. The embarrassment of it was too much for her, and she expressed it always by being slightly irritated when Loulita was around. Everything that Loulita said was met with a huff, and a barrage of advice, that would soon turn into a harangue about the dangers of 'quirky life choices,' and 'living outside societal norms.' Loulitas sister was a mother, which was, in her eyes, the most important thing any person could be; gave her the right, she believed, to condemn anyone who wasn't one, especially her sister. The only thing Loulita could rely on was the aching in her stomach. It kept her from forgetting her place, and her circumstances; from getting naive, saying too much, letting her guard down. It was the only defense she had against being victimized, abused and dumped all over again. If she deserved to drink chocolate, and fill her belly, why did she have no family, no one to love her? Because she deserved to be left out, that's why. It was the only reasonable explanation. Why had her parents died? Both of them? And now Kitty too? Hers was not the path of others. She was here to work, to get money so that she might find a tiny place in the world to hide within until it was all over, a place to be with the only friends she ever had, the ones she conjured up and wrote into being.

The cruel joke was that she thought she had found that place. But it had been another cul-de-sac, another dead-end, that would now require backing out of. She would have to leave this little nest soon, she supposed, as soon as Helmut kicked her out.

People generally thought she avoided food because she wanted to stay thin, so she might wear fashionable clothes. Twiggy, they had called her at school. Ms. Twiggy. She had laughed stiffly along with their assumptions. For Loulita, anorexia was not about being noticed. It was rather the opposite. It was, for her, at least, about disappearing, about the physical shrinkage of the self, about forcing her very being to become smaller, less conspicuous, less visible so that there was less of her for the world to take a bite out of.

People always left in the end. Or you left because you got pushed. Those were the by-laws that governed her world. That was why she hadn't wanted Helmut getting too close, close enough to see the bones protruding from her back. If you let them in, they can let you down. But he must have seen, the sleuth. She looked towards the kitchen. People always let you down in the end. Better to be ready. Unexpected hurt was by far the worst type. It came with a sinking feeling, like being dropped from a height when you thought you were safe. Not only did it hurt your heart, but also your soul. Everyday pain was better, easier to manage. It helped you remember soul pain so that you could at least anticipate, account for the more painful of the two when it came up big. Being hungry was everyday pain. Cutting yourself with a blade was everyday pain. Being let down by someone you thought was your friend, and losing your home, that was soul pain.

Chocolate is for other people, people with happy lives, with mothers and fathers, she thought as she tipped Helmut's mug of hot chocolate down the sink, and used the sprayer to wash all traces of it away. Maybe he would drop it now.

Maybe.

Chapter 23

July, 1991, Brussels

The weeks passed like a slow-moving barge. Gone were the chatty exchanges in the kitchen. Helmut seemed to know that he had pushed into an area where he was not welcome. Loulita deceived herself by ignoring what had happened. Now the tourist season was in full swing. Loulita arrived at Müllers Palais de Praliné at seven, as she always did. Helmut was already in the kitchen, standing over the stove, stirring the hot chocolate pot with a ladle.

'Come in. Come in. I want you to try this new recipe with me. I have made it just for us.' Loulita hung up her coat. Her stomach lunged. If it had been less of an onslaught, she might have resisted, but it came so unexpectedly that she had no question prepared to deflect it. Watching her, Helmut ladled a warm brown spoonful into a cup, then passed it into her hands.

'Now just try a little,' he said. She looked down at the rich, soothing drink, then looked back at Helmut, his blue eyes fixed on hers.

'I can't'

'Yes you can.'

She saw the knowing concern, the wisdom in his worn face, the tiny speck of desolation, a shadow of the grief that clung to him, something that she had never noticed before. He wanted so much to save her.

'It's OK,' he said. 'You are safe now.'

A lump burned in her throat. She gulped it away, could feel his eyes piercing hers, and her own began to fill. He was not only looking at her, he was seeing her. Nobody had ever seen before. She ran to the bathroom. When she returned, he was standing at the oven, poking a rod at the roasting beans. Then the bell on the front door went, and gaggling tourists piled into the shop. There was no let up until five, and then it was time to go home. She had gotten away. But only just. The next day, he tried again.

'Please, you must eat something, Loulita.' She looked away, straightening herself up.

'Oh, I just never eat breakfast, I told…' Helmut did not move. She could feel him close now.

'I know that you have had bad times before, Loulita,' he said. 'People have not always been kind to you?'

'I'm really not hungry… I should get to work now,' said Loulita, swallowing.

166

'Come, sit down here, at the table. I have a story that I want to share with you. Do you want to know a secret?' he asked.

'No, I just want to get back to… ' said Loulita, blinking back the tears, looking down at the floor.

'You won't tell anyone if I share something with you, will you?' he said.

'No,' said Loulita, feeling patronized and asinine.

'When I was a young man, I was in the army, the German army, the Wehrmacht. That is where I learned to cook. It was a harsh place, the Wehrmacht. I saw a lot of bad things.' 'I know what the Wehrmacht is.' He went silent. She thought he would leave it now, but he found his voice again. 'During that time, I was assigned to work in Katzbach near Frankfurt. That was a terrible place, a camp. I was there during the Second World War. Do you know what sort of

camp I mean?'

'Yes,' said Loulita, a tear rolling from one eye. She looked up at the ceiling to stop its path.

'There was a child there.'

'Please don't tell me about that place. I can't bear it.'

'I won't tell you then,' said Helmut. 'I suppose you are a grown up woman, and you should do as you prefer,' he added, getting up to go. The silence between them that afternoon split the shop in two. Helmut stayed in the back, Loulita in the front, polishing shelves. Five days passed like this, then Loulita approached him.

'What did you want to tell me before, about the war?' 'What? Oh, nothing. It was nothing,' said Helmut, his

back to her. 'There was a child there. Thats all.'

'They had children at Katzback?'

'No. Not too many. There were only five or six, perhaps brought by mistake. Anyway, she was a ….prisoner?' He turned to face her. Loulita nodded, and looked at the floor.

'Each day, I used to smuggle hot chocolate into that place for her. It took many weeks before she trusted me enough to take it. She would rather starve than be poisoned by a Nazi. I suppose that is what she thought I was, and what she suspected I was trying to do.'

'Well, who could blame her for not trusting anyone? You were a Nazi.' Helmut looked at the floor. He turned to go.

'And you think I am like this girl, I suppose, because I don't drink chocolate?'

'You are like her, Loulita, and not just because of that. You are to me just like her, so bright, so smart.'

'Yes, so wonderful that I got bullied out of the university placement that it took me my entire life to pluck up the courage to apply for, because my writing is "too weird", or because I'm "old", or too "awkward" or whatever it is that people see in me that makes them feel like battering me down.'

'Weird? Is that what they said?' She nodded. 'Yes.'

'If they picked on you, it was because they knew you had what they did not have, what they will never have. All the greats left university in a blaze of glory. Even I know that.' 'Yeah, yeah. I'm a forty-something year old woman with nothing, and they were jealous of me because I'm going to be the next big thing? They, who have rich fathers, society mothers and big houses, were jealous of me. I don't think so. The fact is nobody likes what I have to say. That's all.

Sometimes, I can't even bear it myself.'

'Is that it? You can't bear yourself? Really? Let me tell you that they taunted you because you have something, something very special, only that you can't see it. Everyone else can. That's why they went after you.' Loulita sniffled, put the cup down and sobbed into her hands. Helmut got up to tend to a customer who had wandered into the shop.

Chapter 24

August, 1991, Brussels

A month passed. The city bellowed with tourists. No longer did Helmut try to coax his kitchen assistant with chocolate brews. Instead, he turned his attention back to his business. For the shop window, he designed a chocolate tower, a fairytale castle, made up of circular fragments set in rubber molds. Loulita used wooden sticks, a bain-marie containing melted chocolate, scoopers and scrapers to stack and weld the parts together, and to add accessories about the base. There was even a door with a delicate filigree figurine at the window. Helmut worked at the front of the tower, fixing a small engine with a screwdriver, a battery-operated device made up of odds and ends that would make the display move around on a base. Loulita had already bedecked ropes onto a drawbridge, and made a chain of tiny candy flowers for it. As they worked, they chatted about the extra visitors, the influx of tourists already on the streets. More chocolate supplies would be needed at this rate, due to the additional purchases expected.

'That girl, the one that you gave hot chocolate to... at Katzback... during the war?'

'Yes, what about her?' 'What was she like?'

Helmut shrugged. 'She wrote.' he said. 'Wrote stories to read to the others at night, to make them happy, like you who makes sweets for other people, Loulita, but never allow one single piece for yourself,' he said.

Silence rang out between them. She dipped her head, and could not look up at him anymore. Then her face dropped into her hands, and her shoulders shook.

'Can I tell you what I said to that little girl when she had nothing left but her imagination because all the people she loved were gone?' Loulita nodded.

'I said to her that it is OK to cry.' At those words, Loulita's face crumpled. She folded down, and sobbed.

'Was it your mother?' said Helmut as Loulita sniffed. 'Your father?' he prodded.

'I don't have anyone. I never have. Both of them are gone.' She looked at him, her face red and blotchy. Helmut stayed silent as the tears came.

'You cry because someone has noticed; because somebody has the eyes to see. Do you think nobody has seen you before?'

She got up and went to the bathroom. The water came steadily from her eyes for thirty minutes. When she unlatched the door, Helmut was in the kitchen, standing at the stove.

'Will you take a cup of this cocoa now?' he said. 'No,' said Loulita.

'I am having one' said Helmut, 'I might have a piece of cake with it, or maybe a sandwich. And then you know what?

'What?' said Loulita.

'I think it is time that I showed you the nine-bean blend. 'What do you think about that?' Loulita pushed dark

strands of hair away from a blotchy face, then she looked

out the window beside her, where a large seagull landed in a sudden flap of white feathers on the ledge. She gasped and pulled away.

'I have seen that bird many times recently. Maybe you have a friend that you didn't know about,' said Helmut.

The bird padded on pink rubbery feet, moving from one foot to the other. Then it looked straight at her, twitched its head from side to side. She watched its seed eyes moving rapidly. Without warning, it shot off skyward, on towards a castle high in the hills.

Chapter 25

Brussels, August, 1991

When Loulita arrived at Müllers Palais de Praliné the next morning, there was already a lively crowd gathered around the window. Helmut drew the curtains to unveil the display, and the tower rotated. The drawbridge swung over a myriad of artfully bladed chocolate glazed fruit, and a music box picked out a tinkling of notes from a clockwork device so that a tinny melody tinkered from it. All day Loulita and Helmut served chocolate to children; mothers, husbands, wives, daughters, fathers, lovers, sons and office workers; placing assortments into black or pink boxes tied with a ribbon. When lunchtime came, they latched the shop door over, and sat down for a rest. Helmut had laid the table as usual. There was bread, cheese, pickles and lashings of hot tea. Loulita adjusted to the quietness and watched Helmut cutting the loaf.

'How long did you know the little girl, the one that you used to bring the hot chocolate to?' she asked.

'Less than a year. Maybe six months.' 'What was she like?'

'Oh, she was a clever little thing, had such a vivid imagination. She used to tell me all sorts of facts that I didn't know,' said Helmut, shaking his head.

'What sort of things?'

'She used to talk about flowers, she told me about a floating river market once.'

'A river market? Does such a thing really exist?' 'Yes, I believe it does.'

'Where is it?'

'In Amsterdam. I found out years later, and quite by chance, that there is such a market in Amsterdam.'

'Have you ever been there, Amsterdam?'

'Yes, I went there after the war, travelled around the places that she had talked to me about.'

'What did she tell you about the river market?'

'Ah, she had a book that she wrote in every day, told me she had re-created in that book a story about a place something like the river market, where every color, every scent and every flower came to life.'

'That sounds like quite a story. What age was that girl?' 'She was about twelve, I think. Maybe she was older, but

her body was so thin and frail by then that I could hardly

174

tell if she was a child or… there was no food, you see. They didn't let us give the… nobody got food except the soldiers. The children were so hungry.'

Loulita looked away, feeling the lump forming in her throat again. She picked up a slice of bread, put butter on it. Helmut ate for a while in silence as Loulita gathered herself against her emotions. He pretended not to notice her picking at a slice. It was the first time he had seen any food pass her lips.

'I had an aunty who used to write to a girl during the war.

She lived in Amsterdam.' 'That's strange.' 'Why?'

'Well, maybe it was the same girl.'

'Oh no, I am sure it wasn't. My aunty left me a bunch of old letters. I had myself convinced that she wanted me to know something, that there was some big important meaning to it.'

'Why?'

'Well, you don't leave someone a box of old letters for no reason, do you?'

'Yes, I agree, that's unusual. Maybe a bracelet, but letters from your pen friend? No, I have not heard of that before,' said Helmut.

'Anyway, the dates seemed to tally with the whole Anne Frank story. My aunt's name was Kitty, and her pen pal, the girl she wrote to lived in Amsterdam so '

'I see how you put that all together.' said Helmut. 'It could have happened. A lot happened during those years. Many stories. Many mysteries. Many lives were sent into chaos.'

'Yes, can you believe I thought my aunty was the pen pal of Anne Frank at one time, though? That's how odd I am!' Helmut nodded. 'As I said, it could have been the case. They were strange times.'

After swallowing his sandwich, and swilling a second cup of tea, Helmut spoke.

'Well, if you have a name, you could find out more about your aunt's pen pal. There are still some records of the... the people that were sent to the camps. You said she was Jewish? Maybe she was also sent to '

'I don't even know where the girl ended up. Maybe she got away.' They ate again in silence for some time. Then Helmut began to clear the table.

'If she got away, why did she stop writing to your aunty?'
'What?'

'You said she stopped writing when she was about the age that Anne Frank was when....when the occupation of

Amsterdam happened? You should look up that girl that your aunty wrote to.' Loulita shrugged.

'You know, she wrote a book too.' said Helmut after a minute.

'Who did?'

'The little girl at Katzback.'

'Really?' He nodded, manoeuvring a crust down his gullet. 'In Hebrew. She kept it under her pillow, used to read it out to the others at night. I gave her some matches and the

stub of a candle so that she could see in the dark.'

'What happened to her, in the end, I mean?'

'That I will never know. All I know is that I came to give her the chocolate one cold winter's morning. Must have been sometime near the end of the war, maybe the early months of 1944.'

'And she was gone?' Helmut nodded.

'Her bed was empty. I thought maybe she was hiding, as she sometimes did that. Heavy boots coming into the camp must have been terrifying for the young girl. Well, by then, she was bone thin, sick and weak. Sometimes, she couldn't move and just fell down on the floor. When the people got that way at Katzbach... they were taken to the...' Now Loulita looked down at the floor, and Helmut looked away.

'I thought she might have fallen down, so I looked under her bed, whispered into the darkness, then felt around for her hand or foot to see if she was there so that I could lift her up. That's when I found her book.'

'You found her book?'

'Yes,'

You still have it?' 'No, I told you. It was written in Hebrew.' Loulita shrugged. 'So? You could still have taken it even if you could not

read it?'

'To do what with it? If I was found with a Hebrew book...' he shook his head. 'You don't understand how it was then,' he said, pushing the air away, turning his head from her.

'So you didn't take it then?'

'Yes, I took it. I grabbed it, stuffed it under my shirt, and took it back to the kitchen, hid it at the bottom of an old stewing pot that nobody used.'

'So where is it?'

'That summer, the sergeant ordered that the kitchens be cleaned out. He wanted to check that the soldiers were keeping things spick and span. He started ordering spot checks on food supplies and materials, to see that all the utensils be accounted for. There would have been a lot of

178

questions to answer about a book written in Hebrew hidden in a German soldier's kitchen.'

'You would have gotten into trouble for taking it?'

'I would have been shot. If they thought I could read Hebrew, then I would have been hanged. Either way, I'd have been killed if they had found me with a Hebrew book in my kitchen quarters.'

'Just for that?'

'They'd have taken me out there and then into the yard, without even a second thought.' 'So what did you do with it?'

'I was looking for a chance to throw that damned thing into one of the oven fires, but there was always somebody around.'

'So you burned it?'

'Let's just say I got rid of it. Anyway, that's enough about it. This old timer has said all he will say about the war for one night. I am off now. Goodnight.'

'Goodnight,' said Loulita, taking her leave. 'See you tomorrow.'

Chapter 26

August, 1991, Brussels

The next morning, Loulita arrived before Helmut. She heated the milk, set the cocoa and sugar into a paste, warmed the cups and got the hot chocolate ready.

'Aaah, I smell my favorite smell,' said Helmut arriving after her, rubbing his hands. Loulita passed him a cup, and he smiled, showing her for the first time the straight line of a full set of teeth, the gapped incisors under his moustache. His neck and jaw were equine, muscular; the body of a man who during his youth spent much time pushing iron. The skin was sun leathered, ashen hair clinging with uncertainty to his head.

'Aaah, Sehr Schön!' he said, taking a gulp.

'And what are you reading? The Scent of Heaven ?' 'Is it any good?'

'As "Hypnotically Enchanting," as the cover says,' said Loulita.

He sat down, lit up a cigarette, blew tusks of smoke from his nose, looked into space for some seconds. Then spoke the word 'strange' more to himself that to Loulita. .

'Strange?' she said. 'Why do you say that?'

'The Scent of Heaven,' said Helmut, looking wistfully out the window, shaking his head.

'What about it?'

'That name. Ah, it's just, well chance is a fine thing. I always say that.' said Helmut getting up.

'What do you mean?'

'The Scent of Heaven. That is exactly what that little girl used to say to me when I arrived with cocoa, when I smuggled it to her.

'Did she?' said Loulita.

'Yes, and now you have me talking about her, remembering things I had forgotten from long ago. Then I find you here reading a book with that name, drinking the same chocolate, a recipe made for her. Odd? Serendipity, you call it, right?'

'Well, it's a popular book,' said Loulita handing it to him.

'And its written by another Pilzerhoff, too, I see?' said Helmut, reading from the cover. He turned it over.

'What do you mean?' 'What?' said Helmut

'You said "another" Pilzerhoff.'

'Ah. That was the name of the man I gave the book to.'

'What book?'

'The book that I found under the little girl's bed, the Hebrew notebook.'

'Wait, you gave the girls book to someone?'

'Yes, you hardly think I kept it. It told you before.' he made a throat-cutting action moving one finger across his neck. 'I was going to throw it away, had it all planned out. My idea was to sneak down when all the other men were asleep, but that evening we were given impromptu leave to go to Frankfurt. So, I took the book with me under my belt in case it would be found whilst they got me gone. They were doing spot checks more often. Must have believed there were British spies among us. Probably was.'

'Did they find it on you?'

'What?' said Helmut 'Oh no, they didn't catch me with it. I grabbed a heavy overcoat from the pile at the door, and put it on, so nobody would notice me hiding it. Anyway, when we arrived in Frankfurt, we were all standing about smoking. We used tea back then when the tobacco ran out, ersatz nicotine. Horrible stuff. Those were tough times. Anyway, there were five of us young lads there on a street corner, all sharing tea fags.' Helmut digressed, shaking his head at the memory. 'We had nothing. Most of us were not even twenty. Too young to have seen what we saw.'

'What happened next?'

'We heard footsteps. Then, a man came walking by.' 'What man?'

'He was well-dressed, a lay man. You didn't see that often back then. Civvies, I mean. That's what he had on, non-military attire.'

'Who was he?'

'It was that Pilzerhoff off the television.'

'What, Tobias Pilzerhoff was with you in Frankfurt?' 'No, no, not Tobias. What was his name again? The fellow

who wrote the famous book about Frankfurt after the war.

Anyway, one of my comrades started to make sounds, started japing, and jeering at him. They shouted names, called him... The Baker... or something to that affect. Yes, that was it.' Loulita leaned in.

'Go on.'

'Well, that was a funny name, so I asked the boys what it was about. Turned out this Pilzerhoff fellow was some sort of intellectual, a writer or something at the university.'

'It can't have been Tobias Pilzerhoff. He wasn't even born then. He is my age.' said Loulita.

'No, no, this man went by something else. Anyway, he was known to have been a translator of languages at one time, bit of a nutter by all accounts.' 'Why did you think that?'

'A person mad enough to stay in Frankfurt, risking their life to document some old buildings as they fell under the bombs? Well, we called that insane. We had no choice but to be there. He could have got out of it, but he didn't.'

'What did you do?'

'The men shouted names at him as he passed. Then I remembered that I had the book in my coat, and saw a chance to offload it.'

'So you went after him?'

'When he had turned the corner, I said I was off to the jacks. Then I ran after him.'

'What did he say?'

'I didn't wait to find that out. I just pushed the book at him, fast as I could, and ran away in case he saw my face. I'd have been shot if he came up to me when I was with the others and mentioned something about passing a book like that around. I took a big risk that day.'

'You did?'

'It was in Hebrew, I told you I could have been branded a Jewish sympathizer. They would have accused me of treason against the Reich if they had found out.'

'So who was this man, this Pilzerhoff?'

'I didn't know who he was. All I knew was that the soldiers watched each other. Some told tales, got extra tobacco or even a piece of the sergeant's steak if they dobbed a man in.' 'So you have no idea what happened to the book after

that?'

'Well, here is the strange thing. In the 1960s, I saw that man again.'

'Where?'

'On the television. I told you. He was speaking in English. Mine was very poor. All I understood was that he had written a book, and was living in America. What was his name again? Let me think. It will come to me in a minute.'

'You don't mean Claude Pilzerhoff, do you?' 'Claude. Yes, that was it. Claude Pilzerhoff.'

Chapter 27

August, 1991, Schloss Ludwig

After a particularly heavy dalliance with Dionysus in the rose garden, Tobias's love affair with the bottle cost him two days' worth of hangover time, during which migrainous darts burrowed into his head, a feeling which encouraged him to put an end to his profligate binging. What was needed was a spell of abstinence from the demon bottle. The damn stuff was not helping, perhaps was the cause of his creative blockages. He needed a change of scenery to break the habit, to take some inspiration from the living world, be amongst people. All this solitude was not doing him any favors, perhaps. He should take a jaunt, a short day trip, he decided. Brussels was not far. He would go for a spin, perhaps choosing a centerpiece for the rose garden to place over the slab whilst he was at it. He had a sundial on a white marble pedestal in mind, knew of an antique dealer, an outpost jumble yard a short drive away. There he might find the very thing, and then he could continue on into the Belgian capital. Why not?

Awakening at dawn that Saturday, he paid a visit to that same roadside garden seller where he roamed amongst the Grecian pots and urns until he found the very thing he had imagined. Next, on to Brussels. After having some soup on the Grand Square, he strolled off the beaten track, went into the maze of cobbled backstreets, stopping here and there to peer into the various shop windows. Whilst he was there, he decided to pay a visit to a chocolatier to purchase some confectionery for himself, as a consolation, something to replace his nightly tipple.

One little chocolate place drew his eye because of a rotating castle display in the window. He went inside, to buy a dozen salted caramel toffees, but was whilst there, accosted by three overzealous fans who followed him in, then cornered him for an autograph. After that, he slipped away hastily, and drove back to Schloss Ludwig. As Loulita served him at the counter, she watched his face, looked at his hands, ran her eye over his clothing. She did not recognize him as Tobias Pilzerhoff, only noticed him particularly because he brought with him into the shop that unmistakable presence that precedes the famous, the wealthy, and others of a privileged ilk. This man gusted in, bringing with him the same extrapolating air of one-offness that hung about the royal heirlooms who had been knocking about on campus back in England. It was nothing immediately noticeable, nothing distinguishable to the naked eye, but something about him made her look him over, made her eyes home in, made them rest at his hands which exhibited the same subtle evidence of delicate idleness as a duke she recalled. The vestiges of Tobias Pilzerhoff were dark, of course, inconspicuously colored. But his coat buttons, scarf, gloves and hat reeked of quality, of being better than that of an ordinary persons, of being the finest that money could buy. His coat was cashmere. But it was not the material itself that caused him to stand out to Loulita. It was something else, some visceral, sublime undercurrent that sang of elemental intrinsic entitlement. This was a man who had not struggled, or rushed, or counted, or measured as ordinary people do. She caught the whiff of orange bergamot, and sandalwood, and savored it to catch the undertone, the one beneath the aftershave. His was the scent of the affluent, of the person blessed with abundance. It told the story of his life, of the ease that had followed him since birth. From him came the smell of refinement. It diffused from his skin, rose from off his hair, even came from his breath and innards. His cells, composed through assimilation of the highest quality of food, carried a scent virtually imperceivable to the olfactory senses on a conscious level. Rather, it rang off him as a distinction that happens within the subconscious plane. In fact, it was not the smell itself that Loulita picked up that day, but rather the aura of it. The impression of a scent was that which Loulita Hirsch picked up when she encountered Tobias Pilzerhoff although she did not know it. His face, she decided, was one she had encountered before. She was about to say, 'You have an account here?' when the shop door burst open and three gangly teenage girls came rushing towards him.

'Tobias, Tobias,' they said as the man turned around with a start. One of the girls extended her arm, holding up a copy of The Scent of Heaven, and pushed a pen in front of him.

'Tobias, I know you don't do autographs, but please sign this copy for me, pleeease.' Tobias grimaced. The girl smiled, and stood away to give him space. Then, all three of them blushed, and looked at the floor. Tobias scanned them. Relenting, he began to scratch his name on the book. As he did, the same girl beamed, exposing braced teeth. 'Oh my God! Tobias Pilzerhoff is signing my copy of The Scent of Heaven. I can't believe it,' she gushed, putting a hand over her mouth. Turning to face the others for support, they immediately gushed back; gassing and giggling just behind her, in support of their leader. Then Tobias pushed some money towards Loulita, shoved a box of chocolates under his arm, and left the shop, brushing past the girls with a brittle, awkward nod.

'Oh my God, I can't believe it was really him. My mom says he never leaves the castle.'

Loulita folded her arms and listened to them talking about 'TP' for some time. They ignored her even when she cleared her throat. So she addressed them directly.

'How can I help you today, girls?' 'What?'

'This is a shop. Would you like to buy something? They ignored her and kept on talking.

'The same chocolate as Tobias Pilzerhoff just did, perhaps?' 'Which ones did he buy?' the leader immediately tuned in at the notion of having a second Pilzerhoff trophy to take home.

'Some of these.' The girl with the braces stood forward, gleaming over the counter where Loulita pointed.

'So, he lives in a castle nearby, does he?' said Loulita, packing up a box of salted toffees.

'Yeah, but nobody is supposed to know that. It's a secret. I only know because my mom knows someone who knows his agent,' said the girl roaming her eyes over the expanse of candy behind the glass.

'I see. It's near here?' asked Loulita. 'What is?'

'The castle?'

'No,' the girl crumpled her face and flipped her hair, 'don't you, like, read the papers or something?' She turned to the others once again, for support. They laughed and threw their eyes to heaven, and one of them said, 'Like, everyone knows TP lives in Germany.'

'Oh?' Loulita responded. At this, all three girls went silent. 'He's kind of a private person,' confided the leader, eyes wide and earnest. 'Writers don't like to be disturbed. Their privacy is everything to them.'

The others again supported this statement with devout nodding.

'I see,' said Loulita. Well, that's OK. I guess I'll lock the door next time TP comes in here, so he doesn't get disturbed by people asking for autographs when he is trying to get on with his business.' She made a curt smile. At this, the ring leader folded her arms, and scowled. With a huff, she flipped her hair again, and pushed a large pair of glasses up onto the bridge of her nose.

'Whatever,' said the girl. Loulita responded with a scowl of her own. Then all three girls pushed for the door, but at the last minute, the third of the group turned around, shaded her mouth with her hand, and whispered, 'It's in Duran near Düsseldorf.'

'What is?' said Loulita.

'TP's castle. Just because her mom knows some famous people, she thinks she is everything,' she hissed through a slick of cherry lip gloss.

'Is that so?'

'Yeah, she has big ideas about becoming the literary breakthrough of our generation.'

'And will she?'

'No – because that's going to be me.'

'So why do you hang out with her then?' At this, the girl tossed her hair, and her entire face turned upward, brightening into a beaming smile. 'Because we're total besties, silly.' Then she flung out the door and rejoined the coterie.

'Like, duh!' shouted Loulita after her, and she heard the ring leader with the braces asking 'Who were you saying "duh" to?'

'I didn't say "duh". That shop assistant said it to me.' 'You told her where TP lives, didn't you?'

'Did not.'

'You so did, flabbermouth.' 'Would I betray you?' 'Shut up!'

'You shut up.'

'Give me one of TP's favorite chocolates, please.'

'No way. Buy your own, big mouth – from your new best friend, the shop girl.' That last part, "the shop girl", was said extra loud for Loulita's benefit. Then came from outside the door a madrigal of tittered sneers that trailed off down the alleyway. Loulita listened, sighed, and when they were gone, took out her copy of The Scent of Heaven from underneath the counter. On the inside cover was a photo of Tobias Pilzerhoff. His biography said that he was born in Frankfurt, that he had studied languages, had worked as a translator, and was the son of Claude and Ingrid... She looked up. He is the son of Claude Pilzerhoff. Helmut's story came back then. In Tobias Pilzerhoff 's novel, there was an unmistakable similarity to the style of the letters written by her aunt's pen pal. Tobias Pilzerhoff. She had met him once, in Frankfurt, all those years back at the church hall evening class. He had reminded her of her own father. Was she making up a cozy pastiche of unrelated circumstances and happenings now? Was she doing that thing that she had read about somewhere; trying to find a man to project her lost father onto? She remembered how Tobias had gotten into the taxi, how he had been brusque and dismissive. He probably would not remember her after all these years. Even back then, he had exuded a self-assured, established confidence, as if he knew exactly the path that life had laid out in front of him. And he hadn't been wrong. It had worked out. Tobias Pilzerhoff had risen to where he probably had always known he would. With his educational credentials, and the fact that he had come from the right stock, was it altogether surprising? His path had been lit. He had made it. Was it a smidgeon of envy that was driving her now to cast aspersions on the true source of his world-famous book? She had also written stories, but her star had not risen. She was, just as her latest customers had so eloquently reminded her, a mere shop girl.

It did seem unfair. There existed in society, she believed, a tendency to mollycoddle writers like Tobias Pilzerhoff for writing emotions well, to belvedere their work, hold it up as celestial poetry of notable standing. The same society downgraded such when they came from the hand of a woman; brushed them off as romantic mush, dismissed such books as ribald. Loulita uttered a cynical huff.

His connections had undoubtedly helped him, she thought. But the book, she had to admit, was extraordinary nonetheless. It was different. He had captured that elusive, angelic quality of neither and both man or woman. He was Tobias Pilzerhoff, the son of Claude Pilzerhoff, for goodness' sake. She was only Loulita Hirsch, a shop girl with no money, no influence, no say. Her stories would never get beyond the notebooks in which they were written, even though she had been 'miles ahead of him,' as a classmate had confided through a surreptitious note left on her desk all those years ago, after he challenged her in the night class at the church hall near The Goethe Institute. How things had changed.

Today, within a square mile of Müllers Palais, in Brussels city center alone, there had to be, she estimated, no less than half a million copies of The Scent of Heaven being read at this very moment. They sat in drawers, on shelves, in briefcases and in handbags. People read them in beds, on buses, in cafés and on trains because The Scent of Heaven remained, even after all this time of Tobias Pilzerhoff hiding away in a castle – living the reclusive life – the most widely read book in Europe, and Tobias Pilzerhoff with it, the most famous writer in the world.

Chapter 28

September, 1991, Schloss Ludwig

Two weeks after Tobias Pilzerhoffs visit to Brussels, the sundial arrived, and two installers carried it through

the grounds of Schloss Ludwig. At the rose garden, Tobias pushed the gate open, and instructed them to set the monument down in the center of the new slab. He watched the men rotating it, conferring with the sky periodically, discussing the degrees of its position.

'How does it work?' Tobias enquired. The man who had sold him the item spoke.

'This sharp piece here that sticks up…?' 'Yes, the gnomon,' said Tobias.

'It must be parallel to the axis of the earth's rotation. When the alignment is right, you tell the time by the shadow cast. See here?' he said, pointing to the plate.

'It will be accurate throughout the year?'

'Once it's been set in the right position, it will.' Tobias hovered around. He didn't like to be told, and felt it necessary to get the last word in.

'Up until the early 19th century, these were the only clocks.' Tobias informed them, but the men had already returned to their work, and only nodded at him some minutes later when they noticed that he was still there.

In the weeks that followed, Tobias checked several times to attest to the instrument's accuracy against his quartz watch. His findings were in concurrence with the guarantee deployed by the fitters.

With the sundial as its centerpiece, the rose garden had acquired a special sort of peace. The ground, the bushes and the trees had settled back down after the upheaval. Seeds were becoming the green shoots of young plants. Anchored firmly into the ground, they pressed upwards now for the light. Nature was taking over again, causing all things to grow together in that most harmonious of ways which only happens in certain places, without logic or explanation, at the planets discretion, the will of some unseen universal force.

As peaceful as that garden looked on the surface, an equally incipient violence was brewing underneath it. A chemical process triggered by the decomposition of those flowers sealed up in the pit. It was caused by microscopic organisms – a biosphere of tiny lifeforms so small that a person could be forgiven for disregarding them, for passing them off as harmless. Because those naturally occurring bacteriua are harmless in most cases, only that in this case Tobias

Pilzerhoff had done his job so well, and sealed that metal enclosing so tight that those minuscule monophonic lifeforms – when they began to proliferate, and to produce the gaseous discharge that is quite natural for them to produce during the process of decomposition – had nowhere to go.

In the absence of oxygen, and with all that organic material pressed so tightly together, an unusually large quantity of effusious gas was created. So much, in fact, that after just one month, the process of decomposition was already causing rumbles in the belly of the subterranean chamber underneath the sundial.

As the antagonistic forces of space and volume battled within the receptacle, it swelled, and tiny hairline cracks appeared in the concrete slab on the surface. It bulged and protruded, imperceivable as the walls of the chamber pushed upwards.

With only solid earth to meet it on all sides, and a heavy capstone on top, there was no alleviation for the pressure within that sarcophagus. Therefore, the fulminating toxins became incandescent as they fought for space, and then became explosive in their quest for release from their confines. Unbeknownst to anyone, there was an additional aggravate, an old services pipe running right under the pit, which would not have made any difference if but that one unscrupulous farmer who lived five kilometers upwind hadn't been improperly disposing of petrol, mineral spirits and other hazardous materials by way of tipping them into the disused drains.

Because of that farmer, an unusually charged effusion of volatile gases gurgled in those pipes. As well as methane and carbon dioxide, a tense incursion of hydrogen sulfide, ammonia, esters, carbon monoxide, sulfur dioxide and nitrogen oxides fraternized uncomfortably together.

The smell in those pipes was hideous. If a person had been unfortunate enough to poke their nose into that sealed haustra, the fog of grotesque awfulness would have nullified their olfactory senses in a split second. It would have numbed their entire nasal cavity, signifying the imminent dangers that were brewing. But since the tract was covered up, laid deep in the earth, and since nobody cared to go inside that sewer or to think to check – because they didn't even know it existed – no-one had reason to worry about the drains, or the stench, or the potential risk, or the pressure that was mounting daily beneath the plot where Tobias Pilzerhoff had built a memorial for The Scent of Heaven.

Chapter 29

September, 1991, Brussels

After she had finished for the day at Helmut's, Loulita Hirsch went into the little flat, climbed up onto the mezzanine bed, and switched her bedside light on. She ran her eyes over the books on her locker, and opened The Scent of Heaven. But could not finish it to the end, and so laid it down before reading the last few pages, because of the return of disturbing notions about its author. Surely, by now those arcane fabrications of her overzealous imagination would have passed. Ignoring them, she picked up her reading, and with only a scant few pages left, soon reached the end.

The plot was arced, came to a high point, and the strings of the tale were satisfactorily wrapped up in the last chapter. The language was effortless, and allowed the story to lead. It had all the components of a masterfully written novel, but something about it niggled her. It was so very different from the samples of Tobias Pilzerhoff 's old writing, the essays he had turned in during the night class back in Frankfurt all those years ago. She had them somewhere, those pages in the flap at the back of one of her notebooks. She dug them out, and compared the text to the book. No hint of this novel's style was to be found in Tobias Pilzerhoffs earlier work.

Tomorrow was her day off. There was a new café in Dinant. She would go there in her taxi, have some lunch, and start writing again herself to ward off this madness. After that, it would be calming to walk down by the cliffs where gulls swooped and dived over the river. Her imagination needed to vent, so she got up at dawn as planned, sat behind the wheel of the taxi, only that the road did not take her towards Dinant. Instead, she found herself on the Autobahn leading to Düsseldorf. It was still possible to turn back, but by the time she got to the next exit, she would already be halfway there. What a waste of the day that would have been. The evenings were getting shorter. There was good music playing on the radio. Why not keep going? Düsseldorf it was then. No point in wasting the best light of the day driving around looking for a motorway exit that she would probably miss anyway. That city was two hours away. She had not been there before. Why not discover that place instead? But when she got close, she saw the turn off for Duran, and thought of Tobias Pilzerhoff, and wondered what sort of castle he lived in. And so, she took the exit and drove in the direction of that town instead.

Accepting the fact that she was being a stalker now, she asked a villager where he lived, expecting to be knocked back or questioned, 'what business do you want with Tobias

Pilzerhoff?' But the villager did not put her in her place. The man was helpful, pointed out the road, mistaking her for a pre-arranged chauffeur, a driver summoned to take their celebrated resident to some event in the city. It did not take long to find Schloss Ludwig. Within minutes, the wheels of the taxi were crunching up its windy drive. Loulita was certain that she would not make it all the way, that there would be an electric gate, or a security guard in a little kiosk, but no such barriers came in her path. She drove straight in, and parked right outside the front door, where she sat for several minutes, the engine running.

It would be too odd not to knock on the door now, would it not? He was probably watching right now from the turret. Then, a window shot up.

'Can I help you there?' shouted Tobias. 'Oh no, I just…'

'This is private property.'

'I wanted to…'

'Look, I'm pretty busy here,' he yelled. 'I wanted to ask you… can I come…?' 'What do you want?'

'I… your father Claude?' 'Yes, what about him?'

'Was he…… did you ever see him with a manuscript of some sort?'

'What?'

'A manuscript written in Hebrew... it may have been given to your father by a soldier...?'

Tobias went silent.

'Helmut Englehaus... he gave it to your...

'No,' barked Tobias. 'No, no such thing was ever given to my father. No. Please go away...'

'I didn't mean to... I just...' said Loulita.

'What gives you the right to come to my home? Who even are you, anyway?'

'I'm Loulita, I met you once at...' 'What?'

'I'm Loulita.'

'Do I know you?'

'We have met before... you commented on my writing once. It was in Frankfurt at the...'

'You people, always snooping around. Can't you leave me alone? You come up to my house in a taxi, flinging all sorts

of accusations around. Didn't you see the signs?

Private property. Get off my land!'

And with that, the window came crashing down.

Hacks, thought Tobias, they would stop at nothing to destroy a person, and nothing was beneath those pernicious leeches. Loulita drove home, a sick feeling in her stomach. She shouldn't have gone there. Why had she done it? What had possessed her?

Tobias stayed low, stood with his back against a wall for almost ten minutes. Sweating, he shot around to look out through the turret window, at last. Where was she? Was she gone? Who was she anyway, and how could she know? A soldier, that's what she had said… Was that how his father had acquired the manuscript, from a solider? It made sense, that story. His father had been in Frankfurt. But this was the first he had heard about a soldier. His father had never mentioned one, but then he had never mentioned the hidden draw in his bureau either, or the document sequestered away inside it for that matter. Where did this interloper get that story from? It didn't matter. She knew, that was the point. She knew. What is more, she had come to his home, come to oust him, or to confront and threaten him. Extortion. That's what this was. Bloody scoundrel!

Something had to be done. But what? How could he shut her up? His mouth was dry like sandpaper now, his breathing shallow, his heart pounding. Think man, think!

Maybe he was going to die. His old ticker might just give up. Think. If only he could get to the phone without her seeing. She was still out there somewhere taking photos, hiding in a bush, watching him, no doubt. He could feel it. He scooted along on all fours, as if a sniper had a target trained on him, and was about to fire a pot shot through the glass. At last, he reached the phone. Settling himself down in a ball on the floor, he took the device down and set it on the carpet. 'Come on. Come on,' he said, as he waited for the rotary dial of the telephone to spin to its original position so that he could turn in the next number. A ringing tone came, and he waited.

'Wilhelm, it's Tobias... I need to see you... No... Yes, it's extremely important... Yes. Urgent... Yes... About the book... I... need to tell you... Something has happened. Yes... Just come... Yes, I'm serious... Better you come soon... Yes, tonight.'

At ten that night, Wilhelm's car crunched up the drive. Now the two men sat in the drawing room staring into the fire. Wilhelm shook his head in disbelief, then looked up at Tobias.

'Why did you not tell me all this before?' he asked. Tobias looked towards the parquet and shrugged.

'The thing is, you can't ignore this now,' said Wilhelm. 'I know.'

205

'If she is a journalist, which she obviously is, you have to go to the press yourself. Get there first.'

'Maybe she is not a journalist?' Tobias pleaded.

'You said she mentioned something about an article that she had written, that you looked at it or something, back in Frankfurt?'

'Yes.'

'Well, there's your answer. She is from the press. Why else would she take a taxi all the way to your home? And even if she is not, she will go to them. With that humdinger of a story under her belt, she could expect a hefty payout. Have you ever seen her before?'

'Don't think so. Don't remember her... wait... Now that I think of it, she did look vaguely familiar.' Wilhelm tutted.

'See, you must have met her at some book junket. These people attach themselves to anyone who has done anything. First they ingratiate themselves by lavishing you with sycophantic praise, then they find a vulnerable point and twist the knife. It's always about money with them.'

Then Wilhelm stood up, and began to pace up and down. That shrewd old codgers mind kicked into gear. Obfuscating rumors by diluting them with a grinding of truth was the best way. He would meet this excoriating conjecture with more of the same, create a smokescreen so that her allegations would get lost in the fugue. He would shape, mold and bend the narrative so that it ended up at a flattering angle. A plan formed in his mind.

'What we will do is this,' he said. Tobias looked up. 'We will have a party, invite them all.'

'A party? Are you mad?'

'Everyone will be invited. Even Stein.' 'No way, not him...'

'Yes, especially him. Otherwise, he will be the first to carry her beastly story, once it gets out.'

'Oh God.' said Tobias.

'You will make a speech, mention casually that the story is loosely based on another story, one your father wrote... No, wait... It would be even better to... Yes, I have it now... You'll say that it's based on a story a German soldier told him. You must get the bit about the soldier in, since she mentioned it. Explain that your father had been working on that manuscript, planning to make a book out of it.'

'She is probably typing up her report right now, maybe planning to make a book of it herself,' said Tobias.

'Trust me, we can fix this, but we had better act fast. If we can cordon this off, approach it as a triage, contain it, take the reins, and deal with the matter swiftly, her article will get lost among a trove of others, ones that we will be at the helm of ourselves.'

'You think that's wise?'

'It's the only way. Where is the manuscript now? You had better hope it never surfaces.'

'Oh, there is no chance of that. Don't worry,' said Tobias. 'You know, this castle of yours, it's pretty spectacular.

How would you feel about having the party here?'

'Sure, why not. But I have a bad feeling about this, Wilhelm. Are you sure this is the right thing to do?'

'Leave it to me. And cheer up, will you, man? If we use our noggins, this whole thing could cause a very favorable spike in next year's sales,' said the older man, tapping the side of his head.

'Thank you for... everything,' said Tobias, looking down at the floor.

'Consider it fixed,' said Wilhelm. 'Now, it is getting late. Do you have a room for me in this old place, or will I drive into the village and find lodgings at an inn?'

'You will do no such thing. Let me show you to your room immediately.'

Chapter 30

October, 1991, Schloss Ludwig

On the morning of the gala event at Schloss Ludwig, Tobias
Pilzerhoff took the speech from a brown satchel, and
practiced it in front of his bedroom mirror for the umpteenth
time. Wilhelm had worked on the draft, then handed it to
Tobias for editing. Finally, it was duly handed back to
Wilhelm, at his behest for the final cut. The first paragraph
consisted of a long and arduous expression of gratitude.
'Friends and fellow writers', it began. Names were
mentioned, several short anecdotes re-laid. A special
panegyric was included to applaud Jeffrey Stein. But it was
not until part two of the speech that the real meat of the
thing came out. The plan was that within that section,
Tobias would wax lyrical about the life and times of Claude
Pilzerhoff, then regale the guests with a tale describing how
his beloved father had befriended a young girl during his
time in Frankfurt. She had lived downstairs, the child of a
soldier, spoke the Yiddish tongue." That motherless child
had crept into Pilzerhoff 's apartment, bringing with her
stories of perfume and flowers, her hopes and dreams, the
contents of a young girls mind, and even written a few
notes.

Claude Pilzerhoff, Tobias would say, had planned to write her story one day, to immortalize her in a rhetoric, had kept those incomplete scraps of paper somewhere. Only that he had run out of time, so it was Tobias himself who had taken up the father's torch. This, Tobias would say, had been the inspiration for The Scent of Heaven , and for tonight's gala. He would then dedicate the event to that girl, and in doing so, cushion the blow of the nascent bombshell about the manuscript's true origins that both of them believed was about to be dropped.

Next, he would read an extract from the book, and talk about why it was his pleasure to invite 'all of you fellow writers, esteemed laureates, and members of the press to Castle Ludwig.' Then he would relay the legendary tale of how the book was first discovered by The Stoics' lead singer, who was here tonight, and whom would then be introduced. That dazzling raconteur would take over then, draw gushes, and swoons as he always did. After that, the music would start, and the champagne would begin flowing, and the gin and whiskey with it. After that, the dancing and the boozing would take over in earnest, and a fuzzy, hazy alcohol fueled night would be had by all, in which the story would be lost. Wilhelm had instructed Tobias to expect a few sore heads the next morning; that one or two of the guests may very well awaken fully clothed on the lawn. Wilhelm knew this because he had ordered extra strong whisky, and had instructed extra large tumblers to be hired. In the event of press stragglers, Tobias was to bring them coffee, then drive them to the train station in the village. They would say very little on the way; be sheepish, and nervous as a result of not remembering all the details of the previous night, be tacitly grateful to Tobias for not mentioning anything that might make them feel worse. Then if the girls story were to come out, 'Oh yes, Tobias did mention something in his speech,' they would recall, 'something about some manuscript.' At least that was the plan, should the worst happen. As a result of his grace, a string of unctuous articles would appear in the papers, ones that would engulf any whisperings that this parvenu who had turned up on his doorstep in a taxi might contribute to. As Tobias stared out the window watching sound engineers, lighting men and caterers putting the final touches to the rose garden, he fiddled with his cravat. A group of people in black were being instructed by a man with a Walkie Talkie about the seating arrangements around the crescent stage. As dumbly oblivious to the rumblings within the earth beneath the sundial as he was himself, they rushed about. It was only six o'clock. Tobias was still fixing his neck-tie and practicing his speech. No guest had arrived yet, and the truth was still buried in the rose garden underneath the sundial.

By seven, the garden had filled up with people, one of whom was a man who wrote freelance for a Parisian literary magazine. Because he had started drinking cheap plonk on the train from Paris to Düsseldorf, he was already rather inebriated by the time he arrived at the castle, and propped himself against the sundial to counter his unsteadiness. He took a packet of cigarettes from his shirt pocket, successfully lit a Gauloise, but then dropped it due to a shake in his hands, before lighting another one. The abandoned lit butt rolled along the ground, and stopped at a ridge where the covered pit containing the manuscript was buried, slipping into a crack at the side, right at the corner where some petrol had just a day earlier seeped from the engine of Tobias's gardeners strimmer

Because the weather had been dry, the cigarette tip stayed incandescent, and joined forces with the petrol. It burned a tiny hole through the metal casing. A few minutes later, a spark fell into the pit, and met as it fell, the mixture of gases inside the box under the earth, causing the pressure inside to increase. Instantly, they ignited, causing an almighty pop, then a bang. Initially, the guests only looked at each other. Then someone pointed skyward, shouted 'Fireworks,' and everyone turned their faces towards the heavens, from where a shower of parchment came raining down against an opalescent night. They did not know at first that the snow was made of paper. It was only when someone extended their hand, and grasped one of the flakes, that they declared that it was, in fact, a text written in Hebrew.

Wilhelm, on realizing that this was not on the running order of the night's event, immediately dispatched crew to clear up the fragments. But there were too many pieces by then floating in the air, and not enough crew to catch them all. Larger pieces – full pages of the manuscript – were now also wafting through the breeze, and only seconds later, people were holding complete extracts from the original book.

One person among the guests spoke Hebrew. They were the first to shout out. 'Hey, this is The Scent of Heaven. Why is it in Hebrew?' Other people started taking an interest then, stopped dancing, huddled into a sizable group, and began inspecting the manuscript to see for themselves. Because most of the guests were journalists, they were a particularly curious bunch, and had more questions than most. One of them instructed others to begin gathering the parts of the manuscript, and between them, they quickly managed to patch two full chapters together. Then they brought the document to Tobias, and requested an answer, but he had nothing to say, could only stand before them in dumb silence, his lips quivering.

Photographers began circling like seagulls. They captured the entire event, and when the following morning's papers came out, not one of them missed the story, or spared the sensational influx of spurious allegations about the manuscript's origins. A wave of gossip, radio talk and news commentary swept a week-long brouhaha through Germany, Europe and beyond.

Photos of the manuscript's patchwork of pages were put together and printed beside Tobias's pale face. They, in turn, appeared alongside pictures of the explosion in the rose garden. One picture would become iconic, a strobe lit band playing in front of a castle's fairytale profile, with snow made of paper fragments falling from the sky.

Within the week, eleven samples from that manuscript had been collected, and sent to the University of Seville for radio-carbon dating, a chemical evaluation for establishing a document's age.

Outside Schloss Ludwig, and leading all the way into the village, a line of cars, media trucks, and onlookers now camped. The rain did not deter them. This was the third day that they had been there, waiting for Tobias to come out. They had arrived when the news had broken that forensic scientists in Spain had proven that it was impossible for Tobias Pilzerhoff to have written that manuscript – it was found to have been written sometime around 1945, some fifteen years before Tobias was born in 1960. Now they parked outside his residence, as the world beyond wanted to know who had written The Scent of Heaven, where it had really come from, and why Tobias Pilzerhoff had claimed it as his own. Even with their vans now half a wheel deep in watery mud, that cadre of media made no sign of going home.

Chapter 31

Mid October, 1991, Schloss Ludwig

Düsseldorf is located at the confluence of two rivers: the Rhine and the Düssel. A small stream cuts through the beech forest on the grounds of Schloss Ludwig and meets that confluence of two rivers a couple of kilometers downstream. In normal weather, it is just that; a stream, but when it rains – like it had been doing torrentially for the past two weeks alluvium, mud, sand, clay and gravel slide down from the mountain, and push against that tributary's banks, causing them to bloat, widen and expand.

Getting the canoe on the water in the dark was the hardest part for Tobias, especially as he did not want to risk bringing a torch. Negotiating the craft with one hand, a rucksack on his back containing a selection of his father's books - he waded into the stream. To read in a paper that his father's possessions had been auctioned off by vultures would be more than he could bear. Only those few possessions on his back would accompany him to wherever he ended up, but still, it was something to bring to his new life. With no idea where that new life would be, he stood now waist high in water packing the canoe, unloading the books, fixing them in place with blue twine.

Even if he happened to end up at the bottom of the black inky water before the night was out, at least he would do so holding fast to his heritage, the valuables of his father, his books. Such was the rationale that made Tobias Pilzerhoff, even in this drastic crisis, hold on so vociferously, and with such tenacious guile, to those heavy books that once adorned Claude Pilzerhoff 's Frankfurt shelves.

The vessel wobbled to an uncertain start, but once he had jumped inside it, and once it was on its way, the loaded canoe moved steadily downhill towards Düsseldorf. As a writer, Tobias had tried, and failed to make his mark, but he had never failed as a Scout leader. On the paddling trails, a lifelong proficiency and love of kayaking and canoeing had been garnered. In slow-moving water, he still knew how to launch a little craft. If he was going to spend two, three hours on the water in order to sail to amnesty, then pneumonia was best avoided. Even in this the most dire of circumstances, our friend Tobias Pilzerhoff did not leave his practical nature behind. That is what had made him a decorated Pfadfinder, a scout leader, the best of his boyhood group.

He looked back at his castle one last time. That life was behind him now. Perhaps he would take to a peripatetic existence, or hermetically seal himself inside some arboreal monastery in a forgotten outpost. Either way, his old life had slipped through his hands like muddy silt. It wasn't meant to be, never was. Now he would live out the remainder of his years in exile; bribe his way onto a cargo ship bound for London, perhaps, or Cape Town, or Moscow, and start again.

When he approached Düsseldorf, he sidled along as close to the river bank as he could. Nobody noticed a man pulling himself out of the slinky waters, torrential rain pelting off his back and head, the mud causing him to lose his grip and fall back several times before he docked himself and stood upright on the river bank, reborn. He could have drowned there, struggling to get a grip to shore himself onto the land. And if he had called out, no help would have come because most Düsseldorfers have more common sense than to go out in weather like that.

He had dry clothes in a plastic bag in his backpack, of course. When he walked into a noisy port bar, the tender hardly looked up. In the men's toilet, he dried himself, and changed, then walked back to the bar, and sat down on a stool at the counter, where he learned of a similar place up the street offering lodgings; rooms mostly rented by the hour. He would go there later and sleep, but first he needed to get drunk, very drunk indeed.

Earlier that day back in Brussels, Loulita stared at a photo of Ingrid with baby Tobias that her aunty had left her. Later, at the central library in Düsseldorf, she searched through old newspapers, and at last came across what she was looking for; a picture of a woman with navy eyes, Nordic blonde hair. Ingrid Pilzerhoff, Tobias Pilzerhoff 's mother, the woman who had written to her own father, the woman that he had been having an affair with, the woman he had visited in New York the year Tobias was born. Tobias Pilzerhoff was not the son of Claude Pilzerhoff. He was the result of an affair his mother had conducted with Loulita's own father, Samuel Hirsch. Loulita drove the streets of Düsseldorf, drove with no thought of a destination, rain lashing hard on the taxi roof.

At 1am, Tobias stumbled blearily out of a port-side bar, and crossed the road. Passing in front of a taxi, he did not see the driver, but she saw him. The vehicle flashed its headlights, and a door opened.

Chapter 32

November, 1991, Brussels

Tobias had not left the bedsit above Müllers Palais de Praliné in a fortnight. He dared not venture beyond it for fear of being identified. Since nobody knew that Loulita Hirsch was his sister – how could they when be had only just discovered it himself — that little roost offered a candid retreat. Tobias's father's books sat on a neat shelf. Loulita had produced the photo of his mother, and the letters sent to Loulita's father, along with the photograph; the handwriting undoubtedly Ingrid Pilzerhoffs.

Today was Loulita's day off, and the day that Tobias planned to surrender an admission letter to the news desk of Die Freizeit to bring the entire saga to an end. No more living a lie, he thought, squinting through the morning sun which drenched the little flat. In that bewildering light, he scanned his father's books in search of some paper on which to type his confession, but his eyes fell instead on a book he had not seen for years; Thus Said Zarathusthra by the nineteenth century German philosopher Friedrich Wilhelm Nietzsche. Loulita looked up from her reading and smiled. She had already taken a coffee to the rattan chair by the window, and was nestled there.

220

'Your father found much wisdom in those pages,' she said, nodding toward the paperback he now held in his left hand. 'He must have read it a thousand times, judging by its condition.' Tobias looked at the title, then perused its dog-eared cover, a verification of just how often Claude had indeed referred to those pages over the course of his life.

Nietzsche had chosen a Persian prophet to prompt a re-evaluation of society's polarized, compartmentalized notions of good and bad in the book. Like Nietzsche, Claude had foreseen a time beyond simplified morality, beyond religion. He had talked about the mangled image of the Übermensch, believed in a time of self development and individuation over religious dogma, over the rights and wrongs of ancient doctrines carved into stone.

Like the Pilzerhoff 's, Nietzsche was German. Born in the village of Lützen in 1844, his father was the pastor of the township. Nietzsche originally set out to replicate his father's career, as Tobias had attempted to do. The only difference was that Tobias had failed, and soon the world would know just how abysmally he had done it. He picked out a ream of blank bonded typewriter paper from a shelf, and considered the book's main premise. Nietzsche had meant, through Zarathustra, to shock his audience into consciousness with declarations like 'God is Dead.' He had believed shock to be the only device through which awakening might come about. Wilhelm had framed and pasted over the explosion at Schloss Ludwig with a similar brush. From the recent news articles that Loulita brought back to the flat, Wilhelm had even pointed to Zarathustra. Strange that Tobias had unearthed that book today, of all days. He had not seen it for years.

Lou Andreas-Salomé was the brilliant Russian psychologist and writer who Nietzsche had fallen in love with whilst she had been committed to another man. Tobias thought of his half sister's name, Loulita. She had mentioned that her father had chosen it, the man who was also his real father, Samuel Hirsch. Had his sister's name come from Lou Andreas- Salomé?

Had Samuel Hirsch likened Tobias's mother Ingrid to Nietzsche's lover, a woman adored by two men? Had his mother talked about Nietzsche to her lover Samual Hirsch, the way his father Claude used to talk about Nietzsche to him? Did Ingrid borrow this book of his fathers? Did she let her lover read this book too? And did he later choose

Loulita as a name for his daughter, to honor the woman who had borne him a son, one that he would never meet?

He didn't want to ask his half sister about it. She looked too content to bring up her lost parents now. But there was a synchronicity, a pattern at the very least. Within the dearth of any other guiding force, Tobias counted that unlikely logic in his diagnosis of the situation, and found himself, for the first time, looking for something beyond himself, beyond his father, beyond the institutional codes laid down as laws.

For decades, Nietzsche's philosophies had been misrepresented, and used to promote the very things the man despised – fascism and antisemitism. Similarly, Tobias had become all that he despised – a fraud, a faker, a charlatan. Except that his denouncement would come to light when he was still alive to witness it, and at his own hand. With Friedrich Nietzsche, it had been his sister Elizabeth who had chosen to become his posthumous editor, and who, as history would later reveal, had acted as the obfuscator of his non-nationalist writings.

Loulita had been misrepresented too. Unaware that selective indignation and vitriol prevail where talent evades, she had been shoved out of university. Once again, Tobias watched his sister in her reading chair, took in her child-like fragility. What would it do to her to see him ostracized? He had never had anyone else in his life to consider before, and she had never before gotten the chance to dedicate herself to her unequivocal flair for novels.

'Did I tell you that my aunty Kitty wrote to a girl?' said Loulita, breaking the momentum of his racing mind.

'No, you haven't mentioned that yet,' said Tobias. 'She was called Anne.' Tobias looked at her.

'It's alright, Tobias. I know about the manuscript. I know where it came from.'

'I never meant to… take someone else's words. It all went too far. I only meant to translate it. I never dreamed it would capture so many people's…'

'I know you didn't,' said Loulita.

Tobias sighed. 'I'm going to come clean, let the world know.'

'Yes, you could do that. It would seem like the right thing to do.'

'Seem like? I've got to do it, Loulita.'

'It won't bring her back. Do you want to destroy The Scent of Heaven and its legacy? Do you want to pull it from a million shelves, and give yourself up as a fraudster in the name of veering towards a resolution on which there will be a million different viewpoints for and against your action anyway…?'

'It's the right thing to do,' said Tobias.

'Hasn't the fight for right or wrong only ever driven division, dogmatic politicking and attacks that robbed people of joy? Hasn't it only ever hindered the ability to see objective reality, fugued complexities into one-way streets of fashionable opinion, then left nothing beyond but the autocratic premise of the day?' she added. Tobias stared at her. He had not yet heard his sister speak with so much voracity before, had not considered that she would support him in keeping the manuscript's origin secret before, that anyone could justify such a heinous act if they knew from where that story really came. Now, the monumental divergence of his thoughts split him like a river that gushed abruptly into two streams.

'Life is not simple, and attempts to make complex matters simple are not always the way forward. Sometimes silence is the answer. Starting a public conversation about the book now by pillorizing yourself will only encourage non-experts to confidently jump into the conversation, and debate recklessly regardless of their level of knowledge, and be heard because they will have some journalist's ear. Such trend-oriented scribblers will latch onto opinions about you if you disclose the truth now, and those opinions will overshadow the work, tainting it forever.'

'But what choice do I have? Should I take the credit to my grave? Live as a fake?'

'Is life really that simple for you?' Tobias nodded. 'Yes, it is that simple.'

'It hasn't been for me, and it wasn't for whoever wrote that story. People love that book. It has changed the world. If you attach a scandal to it, all the good will be taken away.'

'What are you saying, Loulita?'

'Let it go on being read, forever so that it's nuanced continuation may be reincarnated over and over again in music, painting and clay forever more. That's what I'm saying.' He looked at her, but didn't speak. The sudden bifurcation caused him to lose his way in what he was about to do. Forever, he heard himself utter the word.

Her words called for meditation on the value of dichotomies of moral codes within the greater scheme of things. He thought of Nietzsche and of his father again, and of how the illiberal apertures of good or bad were just too narrow. He considered the world as it had looked before, in his father's time, during the last war, when political polarities had prevailed, and extreme socialism and fascism had led the way. His head hurt.

'Think carefully about what you do next, Tobias. Perhaps that manuscript needed to be pushed out into the public domain by someone whose name carried weight, so that it could come to be read at just the right time in history, and keep being read after all of us are dead and gone. Perhaps there is another way of giving it back, of giving it the longevity it deserves, a way that will enable it to be loved and enjoyed by future generations.'

'What other way?' Tobias asked. She shrugged, then walked back to her chair, sat down, and resumed her writing. He considered his sister's words, how she had said she had given up her studies, left England behind, and returned to Germany to take up her old job as a taxi driver, as a result of cavalier manipulations. Would she go back to that work again if things got bad because of his need to morally parade himself now? And for whom? What difference would it make? Was it naive to pillory himself for some noble crusade at this late hour, as she had done? If he gave himself up, and came clean, would he only be martyring himself – and her – all over again in the hunt for some simplistic idealism?

Despite his noble intentions, Nietzsche had been misrepresented, and he had not faked his way to greatness as Tobias had. Misrepresentation had happened to Nietzsche through no fault of his own. In a way, the same poison chalice had now been handed to Tobias. Certainly, he had not intentionally defrauded anyone; had not meant to become entangled in any of this. Maybe his sister was right. At worst, he was a mere cipher, not the villain he was about to paint himself as. And what of posterity? Was it to be robbed for eternity of The Scent of Heaven? His mind segued from World War Two to the reunification of Germany. The world was a peaceful place at last. Nietzsche's work had been rediscovered, and the truth of his works meaning finally resolved. Ideas travelled well through periods of chaos into peace. People were only blips of material matter beside them. Brilliant concepts outlived men and their failings. What good would it do to banish a book by tainting the story with the weight of his own moral burden?

And what would become of his sister if she was to become caught up in this? She looked so frail.

Chapter 33

December, 1991, Brazil

Six weeks later, a man and a woman arrived in Brazil. They had new names, and Tobias had acquired a beard. Each of them had one bag, inside which were notebooks full of stories, the ones accumulated by Loulita.

During the crossing Loulita had written, whilst her brother had read, re-edited, re-written parts, and made additions here and there. Then Blossoms arrived on Wilhelm's desk in Berlin. The writing was declared by critics as Tobias Pilzerhoff's best work yet. A year later, another book came, and the next year another.

As time passed, and the Pilzerhoff-Hirsch writing engine became more efficient, poignant whispers started to circulate back in Germany. People said that the manuscript, the explosion and the photo at Schloss Ludwig had been staged for publicity.

Wilhelm encouraged this hypothesis, adding to it that the entire night had been an art installation, an experimental concoction, a sort of shock therapy aimed at provocation, in the name of critical self-examination. The elaborate event had been a hoax, he declared, set up at his calling in order to ready the journalistic community for what was to come; to prepare them for Tobias Pilzerhoff's transcendental next book, Blossoms. Wilhelm deemed that book a masterfully orchestrated Cirque de Son et Lumière, and few could find a counter-argument.

Wilhelm declared that shock was the great provocateur of enlightenment, that only genuine feeling precedes truth, and that there is no room for rigid views, or polarities, unoriginality, and extreme political persuasions in the world of literary criticism – which was and is teeming with those very things, he claimed. Having spoken to Tobias several times by way of long distance telephone calls, he followed through with the Nietzsche's parallel, said that he and Tobias Pilzerhoff had sought a cultural literary rejig, set out to awaken each attendee at the Castle event, to ruffle their feathers, 'individuate' them by having them bear witness to an epic climatic event, a staged shock.

What it was, he said, was fully immersive satire, experiential high theatre of which only the most illustrious members of the intellectually minded artistic milieu could appreciate, and latterly be in a position to recount in words. Others might not grasp such art, so he had cherry-picked the audience, instead of putting the thing in a museum, or on a public stage. Few went against it, and those who mentioned the carbon dating were shouted down, or cast off as culturally indolent, once Wilhelm inferred that the scientists were part of the show.

The exclusive element – combined with the onus that Wilhelms whitewashing planted into the heads of the attendees – added to the cult status and mystique that came in the years that followed. By the dawn of the new millennium, Wilhelm had well and truly sketched the night as a spectacular literary pre-launch, an artistic extravaganza, a phantasmagorical showcase the like of which the world would never see again. It had all been done in the name of expression, and for the lived experience, and to induce fresh thought. People bought the idea with relish.

Persons present, the ones who had been invited, and had witnessed the event, enjoyed the notion that they had been 'in on something', 'gone through' something, been initiated. It instilled in almost every one of them a sense of pride, as well as an interconnectedness that elevated them above their peers who had not been there. It created a schism, a group who defended what had occurred, and were for Tobias, but also a group who could not accept the story they were fed, and were therefore against him. The group for him were seen as more hip, cooler, and were made up of the younger people. They enjoyed the retelling of the fabricated story, calling the other group 'fuddy duddies.' Some made L symbols with their hands whenever they spoke about the opposing junta. The ones who went against

231

Tobias were branded as conspiracy theorists, and put with the people who look at the sky for alien space-craft at night.

In turn, those that were for Tobias and Wilhelms' claims about the night at the castle supported Blossoms with the passion of persons with something to prove, war-like dedication. All the subsequent books that Loulita wrote, but that came out using Tobias's name, received the same subscription. The group who bore witness to Tobias Pilzerhoffs Castle Palooza wore their experience of the night like a badge of honor, like the original attendees of Woodstock, the hippie party to end all parties. That original guest list communed regularly in bars, played acoustic guitars, wrote poetry, and read passages from Blossoms for years thereafter, reliving the event.

Voracious debating took place within that group. They brought friends to the readings, nascent artists, cutting edge fashionistas, rappers, and others who supported the Castle Polooza Art Project, as it came to be known. Countless extramarital affairs and flings happened inside that group of Pilzerhoff devotees. Four children came of it. People could not be sure exactly who the fathers were. And due to liberal persuasions, it was considered bourgeois to inquire. Instead, they committed themselves to operate as a family, a community, and to culture the lifelong links forged during that time by raising the children within a spirit where everyone was their parent and nobody was.

In 2009, Schloss Ludwig was sold. Recounts of the night appeared in papers once again. By now stubborn ivy had grabbed at the broken sundial in the rose garden. It climbed and twisted itself around the smashed pedestal, and grew over the disk so that only the sharp summit of the gnomon poked out. The original attendees, the group of journalists and critics, met less frequently. People forgot about that little garden. Nature reclaimed it, and it went back quite to how it had been before the quiescence of humans.

But the air of reverence that had developed about that night at the castle survived. Related articles and reviews, including those pertaining to Blossoms were sacrosanct, and ostensibly demonstrated the revitalized individuality of the time, and renewed the value of independent thought. Enchantment with Blossoms pushed it into cult status, and with the proliferation of the internet, Pilzerhoff devotees found its community once again. Blossoms was deemed the manifesto of a sort of new communal belief system, became a codex for new thinkers. And so, it cropped up again and again for many years thereafter within certain artistic circles, in online forums, and chat rooms. Not long ago, the story was featured in several stylish magazines. One did a piece called Flower Hopers. Recently, sales of Blossoms have surpassed those of The Scent of Heaven and it has replaced the former in all the bestseller lists.

A few years ago, a chocolate maker in Brussels received a postcard from Brazil. When he got too old to make chocolates any more, he took the sender up on their offer, shut the place down, filled a small suitcase, and arrived at the exact coordinates issued in that postcard. A man and a woman greeted him, drove him to a villa overlooking a beach. It was here that the old chocolatier convalesced until it was his time to pass on to the next world.

A few months later, sometime in the spring, the first donation arrived from an anonymous bank account in Brazil to the bank account of an organization that deals with the repatriation of looted and lost items of Jewish cultural value. It was sizable enough to cause the accounts clerk to drop his pen. From then on to this day, that same payment has been received monthly, and that same clerk wonders about the sender. He does not know that the transfer is scheduled to continue until the day that both Tobias Pilzerhoff and his sister Loulita Hirsch pass on.

Loulita rarely goes into the little village now near the ranch. She has found a place to be, prefers taking care of the house, the garden, the dogs, and listening to the wind at night. The wind is strong, and she hears trains in the distance.

Tobias takes to the road sometimes, travelling from town to town on his bicycle. People are curious about him because he emits an understated reserve, a quietness. They

234

ask him questions about his life, and about poetry, about books – because Tobias Pilzerhoff looks to them very much like how they believe a writing man would look.

There is a lawyer called Ricardo Santos DeSilva, who runs a small office in Buenos Aires. In his filing cabinet sits an affidavit, a legal instruction signed by Tobias Pilzerhoff, to the following effect: copyright ownership of The Scent of Heaven upon the death of the above named Tobias Pilzerhoff and his sister Loulita Hirsch to be transferred, and made thereafter the legal and rightful property of The International Agency for Jewish Repatriation of Recovered Items of Cultural Importance.

The author in all future editions of The Scent of Heaven thereafter to be named as 'Anne.' The Scent of Heaven to include written dedication on its front inside page to honor the life stories of all those whose voices have been stolen, robbed or pilfered. Furthermore, it is requested as a matter of courtesy and at the discretion of the new title holder to add the following dedication; 'To the delicate, soft kiss of the first day of forever.'

The End

Dear Reader,

If you enjoyed this book, please post a review on Amazon. And recommend to someone you know.

This book is also available in Audio Book form on Audible.

Book clubs and Podcasts

Frances would be delighted to consider talking to your book club or podcast as a guest.

Also consider purchasing more books and audio book by Frances Flannery. Frances writes fiction and non-fiction. You may enjoy The Ultimate Guide to Functional Gut Health

Stay in touch

Go to the website below, and join the newsletter to receive notifications of new titles as they become available or to hear about Frances's upcoming writing and gut health retreats.

Film rights are available. Contact the author through the website below.

Frances also writes under the pen name Flannery Everhart.

Instagram@flanneryeverhart

Tiktok @flanneryeverhart

Thank You

www.francesflannery.com